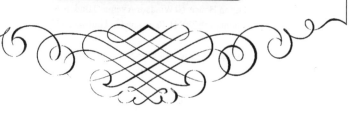

ISBN 978-1-331-01383-9
PIBN 10133585

English
Français
Deutsche
Italiano
Español
Português

# www.forgottenbooks.com

**Mythology** Photography **Fiction**
Fishing Christianity **Art** Cooking
Essays Buddhism Freemasonry
Medicine **Biology** Music **Ancient**
**Egypt** Evolution Carpentry Physics
Dance Geology **Mathematics** Fitness
Shakespeare **Folklore** Yoga Marketing
**Confidence** Immortality Biographies
Poetry **Psychology** Witchcraft
Electronics Chemistry History **Law**
Accounting **Philosophy** Anthropology
Alchemy Drama Quantum Mechanics
Atheism Sexual Health **Ancient History**
**Entrepreneurship** Languages Sport
Paleontology Needlework Islam
**Metaphysics** Investment Archaeology
Parenting Statistics Criminology
**Motivational**

AN

# ANGEL's FORM AND A DEVIL's HEART.

A NOVEL.

Printed by J. Darling, Leadenhall-Street, London.

AN

# ANGEL'S FORM

AND A

## Devil's Heart.

## A NOVEL.

IN FOUR VOLUMES.

BY

## SELINA DAVENPORT,

*AUTHOR OF THE HYPOCRITE, OR MODERN JANUS, DONALD MONTEITH, ORIGINAL OF THE MINIATURE, LEAP YEAR, &c.*

" —————————Yet mine eyes
Were not in fault, for she was beautiful;
Mine ears, that heard her flattery, nor my heart
That thought her like her seeming : it had been vicious
To have mistrusted her."

## VOL. III.

## London:

*Printed at the Minerva Press for*

A. K. NEWMAN AND CO. LEADENHALL-STREET.

1818.

# *Angel's Form & a Devil's Heart.*

## CHAPTER I.

EDWARD was now fully convinced of what he before suspected, namely, the total absence of all honourable feelings from the heart of Charles Manningham. Time only strengthened this painful conviction, and Edward began to entertain the most serious apprehensions for the happiness of Clara Lindsay, until he discovered the preference which she so openly avowed for Mr. Vivian. Too honourable himself to suspect deceit in others, Edward only felt surprised that Clara could so easily trans-

fer

fer her affections from one object to another, for he never imagined that any human being was base enough to trifle with the peace of a fellow-creature, in order to conceal its own secret inclinations.

Edward was now advancing towards an age when the feelings glow with romantic ardour, and his were of the tenderest nature : he was but a bad physiognomist, because he imagined that all men were sincere in their professions, until he found them otherwise. To this generous incredulity may be ascribed his unwillingness to believe the prophetic words of his grandmother, and his equal reluctance to ascribe to the altered manners of Charles any other motive than that of boyish levity. But his heart could no longer find excuses for his conduct, since it had become so decidedly unprincipled, as the gross insult offered to the unprotected Patty too plainly manifested, and Edward at moments entertained a secret fear lest she should even now continue the object of his lawless wishes.

When

When Charles first heard of Patty's marriage, he tried to assume a look of indifference, saying, that he was glad the girl was well settled in life, and that he hoped she would now become more steady in her conduct; for that she was certainly too pretty to have been allowed to become so early her own mistress. It was not every man that would have chosen to make her his wife, after she had become the talk of a whole village.

" Patty has had many enemies," replied Edward, glancing a look towards Charles and Miss Lindsay; " but they have not been able to rob her of one virtue she possesses. And there are *some* who might not have acted with the prudence and delicacy of Patty, had they been placed in her forlorn and trying situation. Ashford was too honourable to take advantage of her unprotected state; he loved her, and he therefore has made her his wife, thus placing her above the reach of calumny, and the malice of her foes."

Charles

Charles pretended not to hear this speech of Mackenzie's; but Clara could not so easily pass it over in silence.—" I hope," said she, spitefully, " that her husband will also place her out of the way of temptation, by not suffering any improper acquaintances to enter his house, filling her head with a parcel of romantic nonsense, which can only make her above the duties of her station."

" Her good sense will teach her the impropriety of trifling away her time," said Mr. Lindsay. " I have always felt a great interest in Patty's fate, and I now flatter myself that she is happily settled, for I have heard that her husband is a very industrious and deserving young man."

" It is to be hoped, Edward," cried Clara, turning round quickly towards him, " that since visits of *condolence* are no longer necessary, you will cease to excite the remarks of the villagers by your *grateful* attentions to Patty, who, as she has no longer cause to complain of her home, and of her

her father's neglect, can now very well dispense with your tender consolations."

"Patty is not very apt to complain of the ill treatment of any person," replied Edward, gravely; " much less is she inclined to betray, even to *me*, who, you are pleased to say, am so pointed in my attentions, the faults of her father. These she was ever desirous of concealing, until concealment was no longer practicable; and as to the remarks of the villagers, if Patty has been so unfortunate as to become the object of remark, it is not among the humble inhabitants of the village that she has found enemies—*they* all know and esteem her worth; the aged hold her up as an example for their children to imitate, and the young take every opportunity of testifying for her the liveliest demonstrations of affection. No, Miss Lindsay, it is not among the *poor* inhabitants of the village that Patty's secret enemies are to be found. She has now, however, secured to herself a legal protector, who will not hesitate to

chastise

chastise even a prince, should he have the presumption to treat his wife with unmannerly disrespect."

Edward now quitted the room, and retired to his own, conscious that his feelings were too warm at that moment to allow of cool dispassionate reasoning, and not wishing to become involved with Clara in a contest which would only render her more and more bitter against Mrs. Ashford.

"Mackenzie looked offended by your friendly advice," said Charles, artfully endeavouring to fan the flame which he saw was kindling in the bosom of Clara. "It is strange that he can be so blind to his own interest, as to espouse thus boldly the cause of a person whom he knows you dislike."

"He was always immovable upon this point," retorted Clara with vexation. "It is the only subject on which we have ever seriously disagreed, and I don't believe that any human being has power to wean him from his partiality for that artful creature."

"I think, however, that he is more daring

ing in his obstinacy," continued Charles, " and less cautious of offending, since he has become the object of public praise. Perhaps he feels that he is no longer under the necessity of being dependent upon the kindness of his early protectors, and that he is now capable of providing for himself; yet, for the sake of appearances, I think that he should act with more circumspection."

" No, no," exclaimed Mr. Lindsay hastily, " such is not the character of Edward: no particle of meanness or ingratitude is to be met with in his composition. I think that he is wrong in persisting to keep up the acquaintance of Mrs. Ashford, but, as he acts from principle, I cannot so much condemn him."

" Indeed, papa," said Clara, " I begin to be seriously offended myself with Edward, since I am well convinced that he alluded to *me* as one of Patty's secret enemies. However, it is not the first time that I have been treated with rudeness on

that

that saucy creature's account, though pro-
bably it may be the last."

Mr. Lindsay, after saying a few words in
defence of Edward, quitted the apartment;
and Charles, taking advantage of the irri-
tated state of Clara's mind, took the opportunity to increase her displeasure by the
most ungenerous insinuations against Edward and poor Patty, who, he scrupled not
to affirm, had only bestowed her hand on
Ashford that she might be the better enabled to carry on her intimacy with Edward.

The poison of these suggestions sunk at
last into the mind of Miss Lindsay, who
began to consider herself as slighted by
Edward—and for whom? for one whom,
above all others, she disliked; still the
charm which Edward bore about his person
and in his voice, continued to keep alive
some portion of that regard which he had
so long possessed, and Clara preferred
throwing all the blame on Patty, whose
conduct she now determined to watch
most

most narrowly. To do this she employed her maid Sally to inform Ashford that the family would take bread of him, thus securing to herself the power of putting him on his guard against permitting the frequent visits of Edward. Sally was commissioned to see Ashford when he called, and to ingratiate herself into his good opinion, that she might have an opportunity, should it be requisite, to caution him against that intimacy, which Clara pretended to believe was no longer innocent, at least on the part of Patty.

Mrs. Ashford did not wish to decline what she hoped proceeded from the considerate kindness of Mr. Lindsay; yet she could not check some secret fears lest Clara had proposed it, and in that case she was perfectly aware that some mischief was in agitation. Sally, according to the instruction of her young lady, always made a rule of seeing Ashford when he called, inviting him into the housekeeper's room, and offering him a glass of wine, when she paid the

weekly

weekly bills. Sally was a shewy, pleasant-looking girl; and Ashford, who thought her the very reverse of what she really was, pressed her repeatedly to call and spend an evening with his wife. To this Sally assented, and thus was an acquaintance commenced, which enabled Clara to be in complete possession of all the movements of Patty, and all the opinions of her husband.

Ashford happened one morning to be conversing with Sally in the housekeeper's room, when Edward passed the window, and nodded good-naturedly on seeing them together.

" Mr. Mackenzie is an uncommonly fine young man," said Ashford, " and as fond of Patty as if she was his sister."

" So I have heard," replied Sally. " I believe our Miss Clara would give her ears to be half as much beloved by somebody I know, as Mrs. Ashford is by Mr. Edward. He was always a handsome, sweet-tempered youth; all the girls in the village loved him, but he could never see any merit in any

any one but Patty Smith. I don't think that he ever kissed any other girl but her in all his life."

Ashford coloured.—" Why, you would not have him kiss and tell, would you, Sally ?"

" No, certainly not, Mr. Ashford, but I don't think that he is very cautious, for I have often heard Miss Clara scold him for not being more particular in his conduct towards Patty. This, you know, was when they were both children together; but they were never happy, except in each other's company; and though his fondness for Patty gave great offence to Mr. and Mrs. Lindsay, he could never be prevailed on to see her less frequently; so at last they went to Mr. Smith to talk to him about it. How foolish! wasn't it? to make such a piece of work about nothing at all, just as if Mr. Edward had been some lord, and they were afraid of his running away with Patty Smith."

" I don't see what they hal to make a

piece

piece a work about," replied Ashford, with the look and manner of a person who wishes to disbelieve his own feelings; " it was only natural that they should love each other like brother and sister, when they were brought up under the same roof. If Mr. Mackenzie, indeed, was now to be running after Patty, or to be seen kissing her, it would be another matter."

" Why, you would not be jealous, Mr. Ashford, would you ?" said Sally, smiling; " you would not deny him a kiss for old acquaintance sake?"

" No, I should not be jealous, Sally, because I have too high an opinion of my wife to be jealous of her; but I suffer no liberties to be taken either with my wife's person or name. I shall always be glad to see Mr. Mackenzie, when he comes by our house—but no kissing now, Sally."

" Not one?" exclaimed Sally, archly; " not one? Oh, you miser! not one kiss more? Why, what will poor Mr. Edward do now ?"

Ashford,

Ashford, half angry, half jealous, yet afraid to shew it, now abruptly wished Sally good-morning; and jumping into his cart, drove rapidly home, with the unpleasant apprehension that Edward was perhaps at that moment in conversation with his wife. With equal speed he alighted, and burst suddenly into the parlour, where Patty was busy at her needle. The suddenness of his entrance, and the strange manner in which he inquired if Mr. Mackenzie had called that morning, alarmed Patty, who asked, in a trembling voice, if any thing was the matter?

Ashford, recollecting himself, drew her gently towards him; and as he kissed her cheek, affectionately tried to calm the terrors which he had so unguardedly excited. —" Nothing is the matter, my dear Patty," said he, " only that I have been drinking some of Mr. Lindsay's ale, and it has got into my head, and made me half wild; I could think of nothing else but——"

" But what, my dear William ?" inquired

ed Patty, anxiously watching her husband's countenance.

"Only my own foolish imaginations,"
cried Ashford. "I thought that Mr. Mackenzie, being too much of a gentleman to
find any amusement in my company, might
prefer coming when I was absent; and
you know, Patty, that I should not be best
pleased at that: for though I shall always
respect Mr. Mackenzie, knowing the great
friendship you have for him, yet it would
be very imprudent in me, Patty, to suffer
the visits of so handsome a young man,
especially as all the village knows how fond
you are of each other."

Patty's eyes filled with tears. — "Ah,
William! I see how it is," said she; "you
have not been drinking Mr. Lindsay's ale
for nothing; some one has been speaking
ill of me to you, only you don't like to tell
me so."

"No, Patty, no one has been speaking
ill of you, nor of Mr. Mackenzie neither;
only that I should not choose him to watch
his

his opportunities of coming to see you, when I am out about my business."

"Mr. Mackenzie will not do any such a thing," said Patty, sorrowfully; "he is incapable of acting unlike a gentleman. I well know how much I am envied by my betters, because he has always behaved to me with the kindness of a brother; and had I been his own sister, he could not have felt more deeply my painful situation, nor have rejoiced more sincerely when he found that I had got a comfortable home of my own, and a good husband to protect me."

"And you shall always find me a good husband, Patty," cried Ashford, warmly, "and I shall always be glad to see Mr. Mackenzie; but you know, Patty, that it is necessary to have a little care of what the world thinks, and Mr. Mackenzie is so fine a young man, and so far above us, that many illnatured things might be said if he was to be often at our house, especially if I was out."

Patty, though her heart was full, assur-

ed

ed her husband that she would always be guided by his wishes, and that if he desired her not to see Edward, she would obey him, though, next to himself, he was the person whom she revered most on earth; for, as she had known and loved him from a child, she would never disown the regard she had for him.

The result of this conversation was but too obvious to Edward the next time that he called, as was generally his custom when he passed what had formerly been the peaceful dwelling of his grandmother. Ashford received him with coldness, and Patty with an embarrassment which immediately betrayed to the penetration of Edward, that some secret enemy had been undermining the happiness of this amiable couple. Edward feared that he knew from whence the malevolence had arisen; but as the peace of Patty was sacredly dear to him, he resolved, cost him what it would, to deny himself the gratification which he always felt in the sight of Patty, and

and only to call on her once more before he left the village, on his return to London for the winter.

Edward, in this instance, however, was wrong in his conjecture. He attributed the altered manners of Ashford to the secret influence of Charles Manningham; but, though the latter most cordially wished to sow the seeds of dissension between Patty and her husband, he wanted the boldness to do it openly, as he had not forgotten the courageous firmness of Ashford when he so ably defended Patty at the cottage, on the morning when he made her the insulting proposal of becoming his mistress. Charles, therefore, felt no very great relish to encounter again the menaces of her protector; he thought that the affair could not rest in better hands than in those of Miss Lindsay, and he therefore awaited patiently the issue of those hints which he had so. liberally thrown out on the day when they were left alone together after the mention of Patty's marriage.

CHAP-

## CHAPTER II.

Miss Lindsay was duly apprized of the effect which Sally's bantering had produced upon William Ashford; and, like the true spirit of malignity, she rejoiced at the success of her plans. Her mind, however, was now employed sufficiently about herself; she had therefore but little leisure to bestow much thought on Patty, who, dearly as she loved her husband, nevertheless experienced many a painful moment on Edward's account, as his absence gave her room to believe that he felt offended at his late reception.

Poor Patty mourned in secret over this belief, for she had no friend to whom she could impart her fears, or seek advice under her present misfortune. At length she resolved to trust her griefs to honest Oliver,

ver, who had always befriended her with
ready kindness; and when next she saw
him alone, she mentioned her suspicions
that some person had been endeavouring
to poison the mind of her husband against
Mr. Mackenzie, and that they had already,
gained their point, since she was sure that
Edward was offended at something in her
husband's behaviour when he last saw him,
for that he had not called since.

Honest Oliver shook her hand with
friendly warmth, promising to do his best
to find it out, though he dared say it was
some of Miss Clara's tricks; for if she had
no feeling for her own parents, it was not
to be supposed that she could have much
for other people. He offered to deliver to
Mr. Edward any message she wished, as
he would stake his existence that there was
no harm between them.

Patty blushed, but, remembering the
blunt kindness of Oliver, she could not be
angry with him. She however declined
sending any message to Edward, who, as

he

he had intended, called a few days after to take leave of Patty before he left the country. As Ashford was at home, his visit was but a short one; and Edward, who had a hundred things to tell Patty, was obliged to content himself with the cold formalities of a common acquaintance.

The winter passed in the usual routine of fashionable dissipation. Clara's extravagance was as boundless as her vanity and self-love; and though her mother's health was rapidly declining, and her father's embarrassments as rapidly increasing, Clara still continued as gay and as unfeeling as ever, seldom passing a day at home, unless when company was invited to amuse her.

Edward beheld this cruel inattention to her filial duties, and trembled for the consequence. Her own altered manners towards himself he generously forgave, but he could not so readily find excuses for her neglect and want of tenderness to her too-indulgent parents. He wished to leave
the

the establishment of Mr. Lindsay, and to provide entirely for himself, but both the parents of Clara besought him not to quit them, since their only hope of happiness rested on his attentive tenderness. Edward therefore remained, 'although contrary to his own inclination, for Clara, too conscious of his filial kindness towards her parents, felt that the contrast of her own conduct was the more striking when balanced against his watchful eagerness to promote their comforts. Instead of passing away his time in those thoughtless amusements which were the soul of her delights, Edward frequently staid at home with Mrs. Lindsay, and by his affectionate attentions softened down the acuteness of her disorder, and beguiled away the heavy hours of long-protracted suffering.

The increasing debility of Mrs. Lindsay rendered an early removal into the country advisable, and Clara heard of the physieian's orders with a scowl of gloom and discontent, as it would necessarily withdraw

her

her from the amusements of London some
weeks before the accustomed time. In
vain she looked for an invitation from lady
Manningham to remain with her family
until they returned to the Hall; her ladyship would not have insulted the feelings
of a daughter, by supposing that, at a time
like the present, she would absent herself
from the sick-chamber of a parent. Clara
therefore looked in vain—no hint of such a
thing ever fell either from the lips of lady
Manningham or Constantia.

The accumulated embarrassments of
Charles Manningham almost rendered his
union with Miss Fellowes unavoidable;
yet Clara had gained so much admiration
this last winter, had been so publicly sought
after, that he felt reluctant to give up his
pretensions to her favour; while, on the
other hand, his necessities eternally reminded him of the folly of thinking seriously of
one who had no fortune. His sister Constantia was on the point of being united
to sir Arthur Vivian, whose brother became

came importunate to have his marriage with Miss Lindsay celebrated on the same day.

Clara had unthinkingly gone too far with her flirting, and had already allowed her nuptials to be spoken of in public, for her to recede with honour. She had artfully permitted the attentions of Mr. Vivian, the better to conceal from the Manninghams her real sentiments; and it was therefore a preconcerted scheme between her and Charles, that each should appear to have fixed their affections on different objects. Clara, however, through the means of Sally, was acquainted with the involved state of Mr. Manningham's affairs, and she therefore began to feel some degree of alarm lest he should deceive her, and, by marrying the rich Miss Fellowes, pay all his debts, and secure to himself a handsome independence.

The cunning of Sally was once more employed to find out, if possible, some of the secret movements of Charles, for which

service

service she was to receive a handsome re-
muneration.

The ceaseless vigilance of Sally at length
discovered that the valet of Mr. Manningham was in possession of much valuable
information respecting his master. This
man, who was the son of a decayed trades-
man, had long testified an affection for
Sally, who, following the example of her
mistress, as most ladies' maids have done
before her, favoured his addresses, in order
to worm out of him the intelligence she
wanted. That done, she hastened to her
young lady, expecting the promised reward for her cleverness.

Miss Lindsay was that evening engaged
to a ball at lady Manningham's: it was
the last that she should attend that season,
as the next day was fixed on for the departure of her family from town. She
therefore retired to dress, in a frame of
mind that would have made Sally trem-
ble, had she not been conscious that she
was

was the bearer of tidings which would make her services acceptable to her mistress.

" Well, Miss, I have seen Mr. Crawford this morning," said Sally, " and have heard such a power of news from him! Mr. Manningham is sadly in debt to every body; but he has found out a way to pay his creditors, though I fancy it is not a new one."

" What is that, Sally ?" inquired Clara, eagerly.

" Only by marrying the rich and ugly Miss Fellowes," replied Sally, shrugging up her shoulders. " When Mr. Crawford told me so, I did not believe him, but he assured me that it was true, and that Miss Fellowes is invited down this summer to the Hall, when he means to carry her off immediately to Scotland, without asking the leave of any body."

" Impossible!" exclaimed Miss Lindsay; " he could never intend so basely to deceive me." Then casting her eyes in the glass, where she beheld reflected the graceful symmetry of her own fine form—. "Impossible that Mr. Manningham should ever think of uniting his fate to that of the poor deformed Lucinda Fellowes!".

"Ah, Miss!" said Sally, "money is every thing now-a-days, and Miss Fellowes has gold enough to blind the eyes of Mr. Charles to all her ugliness. But if he has behaved ill to you, Miss Clara, I hope he may suffer for it, though you need not care, for you can have his equal any day you please. So let him take his golden idol, and worship it all his life long if he chuses."

"But he shall not take her," exclaimed Clara, in a voice of passion: "if she has dared to raise her hopes so high, if she presumes to think that such a man as Charles Manningham would ever feel any thing but contempt for such a misshapen ugly animal as herself, I will make her rue it all her life long. But, Sally, I can scarcely give credit to the information: it was

was but yesterday that Charles expressed his fears lest I should be drawn into a marriage with Mr. Vivian."

" Men are sad deceivers, Miss; and though Mr. Charles may, and I dare say does, love you best, it is very certain that he told Crawford not to worry him any more about his debts, for that he should soon pay them off with the gold of Miss Fellowes. Only you won't mention it, Miss Clara, because Mr. Crawford would lose his situation."

Clara could no longer doubt but that Charles intended to deceive her, yet she dressed her face in smiles, while her heart nourished the most resentful feelings towards her lover and his intended bride. She paced the room for a few moments in deep reflection, then reseating herself at her toilet, she arranged herself with the most studied elegance, in the dress which Charles had praised as most becoming to her; and never had Clara looked more captivating than she did this evening, in spite

of

of the baneful feelings which rankled in her bosom. She resolved to repel artifice by art, and to bestow the whole of her attentions on Mr. Vivian, thus hoping to rekindle the flame which interest and necessity had damped in the breast of Charles.

"This evening will decide my fate, and that of Miss Fellowes, Sally," said Clara, taking another survey of her beautiful form in the glass.

Satisfied with herself she now descended to the drawing-room, where her sick mother, supported by pillows, sat expecting a sight of her heart's idol.

Though breathing with difficulty, the fond misguided parent exhausted her little remains of strength in exclamations of admiration and pride at the appearance of her graceful child. Clara stopped to kiss her feverish lips: her mother grasped her hand.—" Bless you, my darling! bless you! I hope I shall live to see you return!" were the parting words of Mrs. Lindsay.

" No fear, mamma," replied the unfeeling

Clara;

Clara; " I expect to find you better; but I shall not be late. Where is Edward?"

" He will follow you, my love," said her father; " but I know that he wishes first to read your mother to sleep. She will retire as soon as soon as you are gone, and Edward will not be long before he joins you."

Clara bit her lips with vexation, but forcing a smile, she said—" I cannot leave my mother in better hands than in those of Edward. Tell him, however, that his absence on this night will have a very singular look."

Thus saying, she quitted the apartment which contained her indulgent parents, one of whom was in the last stage of a decline, and so nearly exhausted, that it was uncertain whether she would ever live to witness her daughter's return—that daughter on whom she doted to such an excess, that she had not only sacrificed her health, but her fortune, to procure her all those

pleasures

pleasures. which she so thoughtlessly and so selfishly. sighed for.

Edward lingered behind Miss Lindsay, from an unaccountable reluctance to quit her suffering mother, until he had performed his accustomed task of reading to her after she had retired for the night. Had he, like Clara, only studied his own selfish inclinations, he would have fled from the sick-chamber of Mrs. Lindsay to the gay ball-room of lady Manningham, have flown with all the high-raised hopes of youthful expectation, for it was the first evening of Flora's appearing in public, and Frederic had promised to him her hand after the first dance, which she was to open with the second son of the duke of ———.

Although the thoughts of Edward naturally wandered to the scene of mirthful festivity, yet he refused to join it until he had soothed to rest the fluttering spirits of the invalid, whose mind, full of her absent child, refused this evening to compose
itself

itself as early as usual. At length the tender voice of Edward operated like a pleasing opiate on the tired senses of Mrs. Lindsay—she fell into a gentle slumber, and Edward, softly quitting her bedside, hastened to his chamber, in order to prepare himself for his evening's amusement.

Clara, piqued by the attentive goodness of Edward, which only rendered her own conduct more striking, replied to all the inquiries concerning his absence with evasive caution. She saw, to her mortification, Charles lead out Miss Fellowes to the dance, and checking her resentful feelings, she smilingly bestowed her hand on Mr. Vivian, who proudly led her to where Charles and his little deformed partner were standing. The strikingly beautiful figure of Miss Lindsay only made that of poor Lucinda appear more frightful; yet, could a casual observer have seen into each separate heart, could he have beheld the one, all meekness, gentleness, and benevolence—the other, selfish, proud, and malignant,

nant,

nant, with what disgust would he have turned from the finely-proportioned form of Clara—with what complacency would he have viewed the distorted person of the sweet-tempered and amiable Lucinda !

Charles could not, however, prevent himself from drawing comparisons between the two ladies, which were highly advantageous to the wishes of Miss Lindsay. His eyes followed with delight her graceful movements, and he envied Vivian the privileges of the dance, as well as the smiles and attentions of the captivating Clara.

Miss Lindsay read in his watchful glance the uneasiness he felt, and redoubled her flattering assiduities to the unsuspecting Vivian; while Charles, half mad with his jealous fears, resolved to seize the first opportunity of engaging her for a partner.

Clara wisely excused herself from complying with his request, thus adding to his ill-humour and chagrin.

"I must speak to you, Clara," said he,

" or

" or I shall commit some folly which will
ruin me for ever."

Miss Lindsay laughingly replied, that
she did not think that she should have
time to attend to him that evening.

" To-morrow you leave town," replied
Charles, passionately: " I must speak to
you to-night."

" Miss Fellowes is looking for you," retorted Clara, with an air of raillery, and
turned to speak to Mr. Vivian.

Charles at that moment cursed Miss
Fellowes and all the world, Clara included,
for he just caught a glimpse of her countenance, and saw her smile encouragingly
on his rival.

It was late before Edward made his appearance, and when he did, Frederic re-
proached him bitterly for his tardiness.—
" I should have thought, Mackenzie," said
he, " that you would have been one of the
first to greet the introduction of Flora
into public, instead of which——"

" The loss has been solely my own, dear
Frederic,"

Frederic," replied Edward : " but where is your lovely sister ?"

Frederic conducted him to where Flora was sitting, whose cheeks glowed with the blush of pleasure at his approach, yet he thought that her dark-eyes seemed to reprove him for his absence.

" I know that you will pardon me," said Edward, tenderly pressing the soft hand of Flora in his own, " for my apparent dilatoriness on this happy evening; but poor Mrs. Lindsay was so extremely low, that I almost feared that I should be deprived entirely of the felicity of seeing you."

"Pardon you ! oh, Mr. Mackenzie, upon such an occasion, to ask it was unnecessary. I knew that it was not want of kindness that kept you absent. Poor Mrs. Lindsay ! I fear that her recovery is doubtful."

" I fear so indeed," replied Edward, with a sigh of sympathy that was echoed back again by Flora.

At

At that instant Clara came up to them. "Oh, you are come at last, Mr. Gravity," said Clara: "pray did you see mamma before you left home?"

"I staid with her until she dozed," replied Edward, with a coldness which he could not repress, "and then I left her to the care of her nurse: but you mean to return early to-night, do you not?"

"Yes, certainly; but as my mother is not worse than usual, and as this is the last of my winter's amusements, I shall stay supper. Flora, my little love, you look charmingly; let me congratulate you upon your first conquest: the son of a duke is no mean thing, let me tell you—But Vivian is waiting for me."

In a moment she disappeared through the crowd; but her words had made a painful impression on the soul of Edward.

"Miss Lindsay is all gaiety, as usual," cried Flora: "she seems to doubt that her poor mother is in danger; indeed she

c 6

must, or she would surely not have left her."

" Did Miss Lindsay possess but half your gentle tenderness, lovely Flora," exclaimed Edward, " she would be spared many a bitter pang of self-reproach, which I fear is in store for her."

The sets were now forming, and Edward led his beauteous partner to where the company stood.　Flora had bestowed on him one of her enchanting smiles, and his heart felt lighter than it had done.　He looked at lord George, and listened attentively to his discourse.　" Surely," thought, Edward, " this is not the conquest for Flora Manningham to be proud of!　It is not an empty title, a splendid retinue, that will satisfy a mind like hers.　But how many hearts will feel this evening the influence of her loveliness! how many bosoms beat with a tenderness unknown before !"

Edward felt uncomfortable in resigning the

the hand of Flora to another, especially as this other was lord George, who had again secured it before his arrival. He wonder-ed not at the admiration so visible on his lordship's countenance; for who could be-hold so finished a picture of feminine grace and sweetness, and not admire one of Hea-ven's most perfect works? but he wonder-ed what all the girls in high life could dis-cover in the form and features of his lord-ship, to make them so envious of the pre-ference of lord George.

Edward had not intended to dance un-til after supper, when he hoped again to be enabled to claim the beloved hand of Flora, as she had promised then to become his partner. He looked for Frederic, and perceived him standing by a couch, on which his mother and another lady were sitting, whom Edward instantly recogniz-ed to be lady James Osborne, from her re-semblance to the picture shewn him by sir Joseph Rennie.

Lady

Lady Manningham saw and beckoned to him. He obeyed her summons with alacrity, when she introduced him to lady James, and the two Miss Osbornes, both handsome-looking girls, who were placed by her side, and who evidently felt no reluctance to be introduced to so fine a young man as Edward.

" I have requested lady Manningham, Mr. Mackenzie, to introduce me to you," said her ladyship, offering him her hand, " as I shall feel the highest gratification to be ranked among the number of your friends—first, on account of your own merits, and secondly, from your resemblance to a favourite brother, whom, until lately, I had not seen for nearly eighteen years. Maria, don't you think that Mr. Mackenzie is astonishingly like your uncle Richard?"

" As like, mamma," said Miss Osborne, gaily, " as two faces can be; with this difference, however, that the one is blooming with

with health and happiness, and the other bears the sickly tinge of an eastern climate and a broken constitution.".

" Ah, my sweet girl !" replied lady James, " and you might have added, of a broken heart; for I have been too many years the correspondent of your uncle not to know that sorrow concealed has preyed upon his mind, and given to his once-handsome, once-blooming face, the sickly hue you mention."

Then turning to Edward, she asked if he was in want of a partner, as in that case her daughter Olivia was at his service.

This was an offer of too pleasing a nature to be declined by Edward, who felt an immediate prepossession for lady James and her two lively daughters, to the youngest of whom he now tendered his hand while Frederic followed with her sister Miss Osborne.

As these young ladies had not long been introduced, and as they were perfectly handsome and good-tempered, and known
to

to be girls of fortune, Edward and his
friend quickly became objects of envy
among the gentlemen, particularly as the
Miss Osbornes declined dancing that evening with any other partners.

" I think," said Miss Fellowes, very in-
nocently, to Flora Manningham, " that
Olivia Osborne would be a good match for
Mr. Mackenzie; they would be a very
handsome couple, and he is really so engaging in his person, and so sweetly good-
natured, that I should rejoice to see him
become master of a fortune large enough
to make him independent for life. Would
not you, Miss Flora?"

" Yes, certainly," stammered out Flora,
confusedly; " I could not fail to rejoice at
anything that would add to the happiness
of Mr. Mackenzie: but the affections of
Miss Osborne may be already engaged."

" So may those of Mr. Mackenzie."

Flora started and turned pale.

" I do not say that they are," continued Miss Fellowes, smiling benevolently

on

on Flora, whose embarrassment was but too visible; " I only say that I hope he will be both fortunate and happy in his choice of a partner for life."

In this hope she was most fervently joined by Flora, who, had the happiness of Edward been placed in her hands, would certainly only have committed it to the keeping of *one* person, and that person at present shall be nameless.

## CHAPTER III.

MORNING was already far advanced, and Edward more than once had reminded Clara of her promise to return early, but she angrily demanded whether he had been sent as a spy over her actions, or as a Mentor to remind her of her duties? She was her own mistress, and would not be controlled by him.

" It is as a friend and brother that I ventured

ventured to advise you, Miss Lindsay," said Edward; " but I will offend no longer. I thought that should anything occur during your absence, you would not easily make peace with your own conscience."

" It will be long before I make peace with *you*," replied Clara, sharply, " since you have done *your* best, at least, to spoil all my pleasure to-night. But you will find yourself disappointed."

Then turning hastily on her heel, she left him to wonder at her total want of filial affection for one of the most tender and indulgent of parents. In spite of the warm gratitude of Edward's nature; in spite of his partiality for Clara, which sprung solely from that high sense of the kindness she had ever, until lately, manifested towards him, he could no longer find excuses for her conduct—no longer view her with any other sentiments than those of pity and disgust.

At the end of the first dance after supper,

per, Edward found himself so suddenly
indisposed that he requested, Frederic to
lead him into another apartment, where he
might inhale a purer air, desiring him,
however, not to notice to any one his illness. Frederic, with brotherly solicitude,
conducted him to a private chamber, which
had been laid out for the refreshment of a
few select friends of his mother. After
waiting until he saw Edward recovering,
he, by his desire, quitted him to join the
gay party in the ball-room, his friend promising to follow in a few minutes.

The sudden indisposition of Edward
proceeded 'from the lively badinage of the
Miss Osbornes, who were remarking to
each other the pointed behaviour of lord
George to Flora Manningham.—" What
a lovely little creature she is !" exclaimed
Maria ; " so sweet tempered, so unassum-
ing, that she shrinks from the general admiration which she has so justly excited.
If his lordship is not deeply enamoured, I
will never again pretend to read the lan-
guage

guage of the eyes, or to be any judge of
what is passing within the mind."

" He is of too much consequence to be
rejected," said Olivia, " by lady Manningham; therefore we may conclude that Flora
will in all due time become lady George
——."

Edward turned sick; and feeling that
he looked pale, and that his limbs refused
to support his body, he thought it most
prudent to retire for a short time, lest his
change of look and manner should create
a suspicion of what he wished to conceal
from all the world. When alone, he re-
proached himself severely for having dared
to raise his thoughts to one so much his
superior. But that mysterious feeling,
within his breast, which had so often been
awakened, now revived with fresh energy,
and a something seemed to whisper to him,
that the blood which flowed within his veins
was as noble as that of the Manninghams.
The heart of Edward cherished with fond
credulity this singular hope, which his better

ter judgment rejected, as vain and delusive.

Edward was on the point of rising from the couch on which he reclined, when the door of the room was hastily opened, and two persons entered, and placed themselves on a sofa near it. That part of the room where Edward sat was partly thrown into that dim obscurity which renders indistinct whatever objects may be involved within its shade, and Edward was therefore unseen by the persons, who now began to converse with mutual warmth. Honour bade him to rise; but the voice, the words of Clara Lindsay rivetted him to the seat.—"I may save her from ruin," thought Edward, and that thought forbade his discovering himself.

" What right have you to reproach *me* with infidelity," exclaimed Clara, angrily, " when *you* set me an example of deceit and treachery ? Who was the first to advise dissimulation, and to counsel me to delude the unsuspecting Vivian by a shew.

of

of kindness which at the beginning was only meant to be transient?—who but yourself, Charles? and now you blame me, because the constant affection of this honourable young man has called forth a return."

"Then you actually acknowledge that you love Mr. Vivian," said Charles, furiously; "and that, forgetful of your oft-repeated protestations of tenderness for me, you are ready to become his wife?"

"And why not?" replied Clara, with well-dissembled indifference—"why not, Mr. Manningham, when, equally forgetful of your vows to me, you are ready to bestow your plighted hand on the rich and *beautiful* Lucinda Fellowes?"

"By Heavens, this is *too* much!" cried Charles. "How came you acquainted with my secret movements?—who told you that I meant to marry Miss Fellowes? or, if I did, what but urgent necessity could drag me into so hateful, so galling a yoke?"

"In

" In that case, what did your generosity intend to make of *me* ?" said Clara, fixing on him a look of firm inquiry. " Did your humanity lead you to engage for me the situation of humble companion, to your purse-proud wife? Oh, Charles! Charles! I am no longer the dupe of promises, which I see now you never intended to perform." . . . . . . . . . . . . . .

" By all that is most sacred to my soul, I swear," cried Charles, " that, notwithstanding my embarrassments, have driven me to distraction—notwithstanding they have pointed out to me the only means of being saved from destruction, by sacrificing myself to Miss Fellowes, my heart is as madly devoted to my adored Clara as ever! I feel that I cannot exist without you— that I could never live to behold you the wife of another. Will you, therefore, forgive me, lovely Clara?—will you forget that I ever, in the remotest way, intended to violate my faith to you ?"

" I may forgive you, Charles," replied
Miss

Miss Lindsay, softening her voice and look to their accustomed sweetness, "because I feel that I cannot nourish long any resentment towards *you*. But I will not deceive you into a belief that I can place any future confidence in your word. There is only one way now for you to make me any reparation for the pangs I have endured on your account: if you refuse this, I shall immediately give my hand to Mr. Vivian."

Edward writhed again with the agony of suppressed emotion. Was it possible that human nature could be so premeditately base?—that the heart which professed attachment for one could coldly trifle with the happiness of another? Edward now learned that such duplicity *was* possible, and he inwardly groaned at the knowledge which he had thus painfully acquired.

"I understand you," said Charles, "and will immediately give you the strongest proof that I am able to give you of my affection. Crawford shall instantly

procure

procure a chaise-and-four, which will convey us to Scotland; and should my father
refuse to pay my debts, we must console
ourselves with a temporary exile from England, until they are liquidated by other
means. Say, dearest Clara, are you satisfied?"

The reply of Miss Lindsay called forth
the most passionate exclamations from
Charles, who, tenderly embracing her,
thanked her for her kind consent to his
wishes; then rising, he proposed to go and
dispatch Crawford for the conveyance
which was to conduct him to the summit
of his felicity.

Edward, astonished, and scarcely believ-
ing it possible that Clara, at a moment like
this, should consent to quit her fond, her
dying mother, gave a groan of horror as
Charles left the chamber. The sound
reached the ear of Clara; she started, and
looking fearfully round the room, perceived, at the furthest end, the well-known
form of Edward, who, rising hastily, ap-

proached the couch on which she sat in fear
and trembling for the result of their interview.

"You have overheard our conversation,
Edward," said she—"by what means I
know not. Do you intend to betray me?"

"No," replied Edward, firmly—"it is
not in my nature to betray the failings of
any one; but if I still possess any influence over you, let me conjure you, by all
that is sacred, to consider well before you
take so rash, so fatal a step. Think, I be-
seech you, of what will be the hopeless
agony of the amiable Mr. Vivian, when he
finds that you have abandoned him for another—think of the exhausted state of
your doting mother—think how precari-
ous her life, how doubtful indeed her recovery; and when you reflect upon what
will be her tortures at learning your absence, and upon the effect which such evident want of feeling and affection may have
upon her in her present condition, let that
prevent you from performing so rash a
promise.

promise. Wait, I entreat of you, dear Miss Lindsay, wait until your poor mother is out of danger.".

" I cannot, dare not take your advice, Edward," said Clara, a little moved by his voice and manner. "Delay in this in-stance would be fatal to me; to-morrow even would give Manningham too much time for reflection, and the gold of Lucin-da would overbalance my personal attrae-tions. I must take him at his word, or I shall never become his wife."

" And can you hope for happiness in a union of this hurried nature?" asked Ed-ward, mournfully; " will your delicacy be satisfied with so variable a heart? Oh, Clara! that you would but listen to the advice of him whom you once honoured with your regard, that you would but post-pone this ill-judged marriage! The bless-ings of Heaven can never follow the fly-ing footsteps of a daughter, who abandons to the care of strangers the couch of her suffering parent."

" I will

···" I will hear you no more," exclaimed Clara, rising. " My mother will yet live to receive and welcome my return. I cannot now retract—or, if I could, I would not. Adieu! to your care and tenderness I commit my mother. Tell her that my absence will be short; and say to my father that he shall hear from me the moment that I am become the bride of Manningham."

Clara had vanished before Edward had power to stay her departure, yet, with the hope that he might still prevent the ruin he foresaw, and save her parents the pang of knowing her unworthiness, he hurried after her, passing rapidly through all the illuminated apartments, with the generous wish of snatching her, ungrateful as she was, from what he felt would bring on inevitable misery: but Clara, in leaving the room, had been joined by Charles, who, without allowing her time to speak, had conveyed her down a back staircase to the place where Crawford had stationed a chaise-

chaise-and-four, under the firm belief that his master was going to elope with the wealthy Miss Fellowes. Nor was this pleasing hope abandoned until the travellers halted for some slight refreshment, when the beautiful form of Clara too quickly discovered to the astonished Crawford his sad mistake. He gave a sigh of commiseration at what he knew would be the fate of her whom he deemed to be the victim of his master's misguided fondness—a sigh of which Clara was wholly unworthy.

Edward was met in his fruitless search after Miss Lindsay by Flora, who inquired, with smiling sweetness, where he had contrived to hide himself, for that she had not seen him for some time, and had begun to apprehend that he was unwell. The gentle and endearing softness of her manners calmed, for a moment, the agitated feelings of Edward, who, after expressing his gratitude for her kind solicitude concerning him, confessed that he had been obliged to retire from indisposition. He then

asked

asked if she had seen Miss Lindsay; but Flora, who had just left the only room which he had not minutely examined, declared that she had missed both her brother Charles and Miss Lindsay ever since the first dance after supper.

At that moment Frederic came up, and gave into the hand of Edward a note from Mr. Lindsay, requesting that he and Clara would return immediately, as Mrs. Lindsay was considerably worse.—" For Heaven's sake! dear Frederic," said he, " let her be instantly sought for, or it may be too late for her to receive her mother's blessing."

" Fly, dear Mr. Mackenzie!" cried Flora, while her eyes filled with tears, " fly and assure her parents that she shall follow you immediately. Perhaps she is with Constantia and Miss Fellowes."

Flora darted into the next apartment; but the blood of Edward chilled to his very heart, for he felt that her search would be as fruitless as his own. In a con-

flict

flict of feelings, which nearly deprived him of all exertion, he hastened down stairs; nor had he at all regained his composure when he arrived at the house of his friend and protector.

"My God! where is Clara? what has become of her?" exclaimed Mr. Lindsay, as he met Edward on the landing-place. "Her mother, I fear, is dying."

Edward passed him, and advanced softly to the bedside.

"My child! my darling!" murmured the sufferer, extending her parched hand, and languidly opening her eyes—"where is my beloved Clara? will she not come to receive my last adieu—my last fond prayer for her happiness?—Where is my child?"

Edward entreated Mrs. Lindsay to compose herself, assuring her that Clara would follow him as soon as she was informed of her father's note.

"I did not expect, Edward, that you would come without my daughter," said Mr. Lindsay, half reproachfully, "when

you

you knew that her immediate return was
wished for by her mother."

Edward felt the awkwardness of his situation, yet, wishing that the blame of her
absence might fall on him, he replied that
he expected her every minute; but that he
had been so anxious to hasten home, that
he had not spoken to her himself, but had
commissioned Frederic to impart to her
the request of her father.

Mr. Lindsay answered, with some aspe-
rity, that he ought to have sought for her
himself, but that he would dispatch another message to lady Manningham, who,
he doubted not, would be more attentive
to his wishes.

" Do not leave me, Edward, dear Edward," faintly articulated Mrs. Lindsay;
" for though my own dearest treasure has
unkindly neglected me, you, Edward, have
been always a son to me, and have loved
me with the tenderness of a son." She
pressed his hand as tears of affection and
sorrow dimmed his eyes. The physician
entered;

entered; Edward watched his countenance, and read that no hope remained. Under this painful conviction, he fervently prayed to Heaven that Mrs. Lindsay might be spared in her last moments the agony of learning that her child had abandoned her.

Mr. Lindsay, half distracted, dispatched another messenger after his daughter. Every sound, every movement in the chamber, awakened the attention of his wife, who once more, in a still fainter voice, inquired for her unworthy child. To speak had now become difficult to Mrs. Lindsay, but nature made an effort to express the maternal feelings which pressed on her heart.

" My strength is going fast," said she, motioning to Edward, who bent over her in silent affliction, as he supported her in his arms; " I feel that I am going to that world where all our actions will be judged. If I have erred by my too-partial fondness for my child—if I have fixed my affections too much upon the darling of

my

my soul, and by this have offended my
Creator, may my present sufferings, my
present consciousness of misplaced love,
expiate my offence! 'Tell my thoughtless child, that her dying mother, in her
last moments, still called down blessings
upon her head—still prayed that Provi-
dence would shield her dear bosom from
those pangs which now I feel.   Oh, Clara!
my child! my child! why are you not near
me, to receive my parting kiss, my last fare-
well?"

Mr. Lindsay begged that she would
compose herself, assuring her that Clara
would be with her in a few minutes.

The  dying  mother  shook  her  head—
" We  do  not  meet  again  in  this  world,"
said she, feebly.   Then, smiling tenderly
on her husband and Edward, who each
held a hand, she, with extreme difficulty
of breathing, besought the latter not to de-
sert her beloved partner in the hour of his
distress, but ever to regard him as a father
and a friend.—" I die happy," said she,
" assured

"¹assured that Edward will always be to you what he has ever been to me—a dutiful and affectionate son. Bless you, dear Edward!—bless you, beloved Lindsay!—bless you——" Clara she would have said, but exhausted nature had performed her task, and the weary spirit now quitted its frail and earthly tenement, to inhabit a purer and a better world.

## CHAPTER IV.

It is more easy to imagine than to describe the distraction of Mr. Lindsay, on finding that his daughter had eloped with Mr. Manningham.—" I could have forgiven her," said he, " any act of ingratitude towards myself; but to abandon her mother—and such a mother, and upon her deathbed!—Oh! of what materials can her heart be composed, who could fling her-

self

self into the arms of a lover—who could think of happiness, when the tenderest of parents was breathing her last?"

"Miss Lindsay did not believe that her mother was in danger," replied Edward, wishing to soften down the poignancy of her father's feelings, although his own heart did not admit any excuse for her conduct, " and it is but charitable in us to suppose that the persuasions of Mr. Manningham overruled all her filial scruples, and silenced her objections."

Mr. Lindsay shook his head in mournful incredulity.—" Seek not to lighten her crime, my dearest Edward," said he; "seek not to palliate a fault of the blackest kind —a fault which you are incapable of committing, and at which your nature must revolt. Her poor mother, as well as myself, sacrificed for her our own comforts, our own peace and tranquillity—to procure her wishes, we launched into pleasures but ill suited to our finances; yet for her sake we bore our embarrassments patiently,

little

little expecting so cruel a return for all our misplaced, our prodigal affection. Oh, Clara! if at a future time Heaven ever bestows on you the sacred name of mother, *then*, and not till *then*, will you know the pang, the deep, the remediless agony caused by an ungrateful child."

Edward, had it been possible, would fain have attempted to excuse the conduct of Miss Lindsay, but he felt how vain, how futile was even the wish to throw a veil over actions like hers. With sorrow, such as might well become the grateful soul of Edward, he followed to the grave the remains of Mrs. Lindsay ; and as the cold earth obscured her coffin from his sight, as he heard the long-drawn sob of anguish which burst from the bosom of her husband—anguish rendered doubly keen by the unnatural desertion of his only child, Edward vowed, in the presence of his Creator, never to abandon the afflicted mourner during his severe distress, but to remain with him, whatever might be his fate, and to be to him what

his

his ungrateful Clara should have been—the
comforter and soother of his declining
years.

Mr. Lindsay was almost too deeply ab-
sorbed in the consciousness of the loss he
had sustained, to look into his own deranged affairs, or even to converse much
on a subject which forcibly recalled to his
memory the conduct of his once-idolized
daughter. He felt, however, the strong
necessity of making the whole of his embarrassments known to Edward, who,
though only now in his eighteenth year,
was fully capable of being serviceable to
him in this painfully important business.
Edward, unasked, unsolicited, had promised not to leave him, and had volunteered
to perform all the little delicate and tender
offices of a son; Mr. Lindsay therefore
made an effort to rouse himself one evening after the funeral, and endeavoured to
gain sufficient composure to speak on the
subject of his own deranged circumstances;
but the remembrance of *her* for whose selfish

ish pleasures he had thus involved himself, and become reduced to comparative beggary, overpowered him, and he was obliged to stop repeatedly during the necessary exposure of his affairs.

Edward listened with surprise and grief to the avowal of Mr. Lindsay's paternal imprudence. He was astonished at the magnitude of his debts, and the number of his creditors; and when the deserted father with tearful eyes grasped his hand, when he besought him to think and to act as if he were in reality his own son, Edward's heart seemed to fill with redoubled tenderness towards him; and he again assured him that he would never leave him nor forsake him, but that he should be to him what he had ever been in the days of his prosperity—a father and a friend.

A little tranquillized by the tenderness of Edward, which Mr. Lindsay knew well he could depend on, he now proceeded to express his wish that Edward would discharge the servants, and that he would accompany

company him into the country, where he proposed to sell the furniture, and every thing that was valuable, to discharge a part of his debts—"That task performed," said he, "my conscience will be more at rest. I do not wish to keep a guinea to myself. My future wants will be moderate; and as I have an annuity of forty pounds a-year, I must confine them within that narrow scale, for never again while I live will I involve myself in debt."

Edward, who wished to continue in London, that he might be near sir Joseph Rennie, proposed to Mr. Lindsay that he should walk with him to view the apartments of Mrs. Alexander Mackenzie, which were then vacant, and which, as they could be accommodated with a neat drawing-room and two bed-chambers, he thought would suit them, especially as Edward knew that the terms were moderate, and that every thing would be done that lay in the power of the kind-hearted widow to make them comfortable. Mr. Lindsay consented,

consented, more from an inclination to oblige Edward than from any interest which he felt to see the rooms, as all places were alike to him, who no longer felt existence bearable.

The name of Lindsay was a passport to the favour of Mrs. Alexander Mackenzie. She had heard Edward speak of the family in terms of grateful affection, and she therefore felt an immediate desire to perform every friendly attention towards the widowed friend of her young favourite. She knew also that with Mrs. Lindsay expired the fortune which had supported her family in opulence, and she therefore felt doubly inclined to shew every respect to Mr. Lindsay, who was thus suddenly exposed to so sad a change. It was soon settled that Edward and his once-generous patron should become the inmates of her house, which she promised should be ready for their reception on their return from the country:

Edward found no difficulty in discharging

ging the domestics of Mr. Lindsay, who were glad to remove from a master whom adversity had already claimed. Sally, the attendant of Clara, was extremely piqued at being left behind by her mistress, who, she imagined, had treated her very ill, in not confiding to her the secret of her intended elopement. She therefore resolved not to serve her again, but to go down, at the request of Mr. Lindsay, to his country-house, to prepare the way for his return, and then she could apply to Ashford and his wife, who, she doubted not, would assist her in getting another situation.

Honest Oliver was not so easily dismissed; he was the only one out of several servants who entreated to remain, and share the fallen fortunes of his master. With tears he earnestly besought Edward not to turn him away, assuring him that he was willing to stay for nothing, if he would but retain him about his person. Edward, who from a boy was uncommonly attached to Oliver, felt most keenly the necessity which

which constrained him to separate from so valuable, so faithful a creature.

" If I could keep you, Oliver," said he, " I would not hesitate a moment to have you with me. You should belong to me, and I would joyfully repay your services; but to deceive you would be cruel, Oliver. You know the state of Mr. Lindsay's circumstances; you know also that I have no resources but what I gain by my own exertions. Those I must now redouble for the sake of your master, who was a kind and generous friend to me when my poor old grandmother died. But for his tenderness, his humanity, I then should have wanted a home; and now it is, thank Heaven! in my power to repay a part of his paternal goodness by contributing to his future support. To add to his limited comforts, I must be economical, Oliver; and though it will give me the most serious uneasiness to part from you, yet I am compelled to sacrifice inclination to a sense

of

of duty. We must part, Oliver, at least for the present."

Oliver could not conceal his tears.— " Well, Mr. Edward, if it must be so, it must; but since I lost my poor father, I have not had so hard a trial as this. Pardon me, Mr. Edward, but I loved you from the first day, nay hour of your coming to live at my master's ; and I do think that I liked Miss Clara better after that, because she was always kind to you when she was plaguing other people to death. But if we must part, Mr. Edward, do pray let me stay with you until I get another situation. I won't be any trouble, any hindrance to you at all; only do pray let me stay with you until I get another place." Edward could not object to this request, which enabled him to retain about his person, at least for a short time longer, a being who so sincerely loved him, and to whom he was equally attached. He accordingly paid him what was due of his wages,

wages, saying at the same time, that, until their return from the country, and until Oliver had obtained for himself a comfortable situation, he should consider himself as alone responsible for his wages.

" God bless you! and thank you, dear Mr. Edward!" cried honest Oliver, joyfully. " I wants no wages; I only ask to see your happy face, to hear your kind and encouraging voice. I never saw but one face, never heard but one voice except yours, which had the same effect on me."

" And whose was that, Oliver?" inquired Edward, scarce knowing that he did do so.

" Why, Miss Flora at the Hall," replied Oliver. " I could almost swear that you were cut out for each other, for when either of you smile, you are so like each other; and Patty Ashford says the same."

" Does she?" hastily exclaimed Edward; then, checking the rapturous feelings of the moment, he said—" It can only be in your imaginations, Oliver, for there exists

no

no real resemblance between me and Miss Manningham."

-: Edward felt it necessary to call on lady Manningham the day before he left town, as he had not seen any of the family since the night of the ball. Mr. Lindsay, had received a letter from Clara, who, as a mere matter of form, begged pardon for the step she had taken, hoped that her mother's accustomed tenderness would find excuses for her flight, and promised to hasten her return as soon as she became Mrs. Manningham. Mr. Lindsay, with the just feelings of an insulted father, declined answering this last proof of Clara's cold-blooded selfishness; yet he dictated to Edward a few hnes, merely to inform his daughter, that the mother, on whose tenderness she relied as usual for pardon, was no more—that she had died on the night of her elopement. Mr. Lindsay requested Edward to be silent on every other subject, as he did not wish to intrude his sorrows on the notice of one who had so clearly proved her utter incapability of feeling for any but herself.

— Edward, for the first time, experienced a reluctance to call at the house of sir Charles Manningham. He had heard twice from Frederic since the death of Mrs. Lindsay, but he was the only one of his family who had taken the slightest notice of him since the elopement of Clara; and from him he learnt that both his parents were extremely incensed at Charles for concealing his attachment, and for marrying without their consent. Edward, notwithstanding his reluctance, thought that it was a mark of respect which they deserved from him, and he accordingly bent his steps towards the mansion of sir Charles.

Frederic and Flora were alone in the drawing-room when Edward was announced. The former flew to greet him with extended hand, while the changeful countenance of the latter, although she was silent, expressed her ready participation in the sentiments of her brother.

" Mackenzie,"

" Mackenzie," said Frederic, " I rejoice to see you. I hope that you will remain until my father and mother come back— I hope that you will clear yourself from all knowledge of this unlucky affair. I have fought boldly for you, my friend, in your absence; I have never flinched, never yielded an inch of ground—have I, Flora? No, though all seem inclined to believe that you knew of the intended elopement, yet I have defended you through thick and thin, declaring my positive assurance that you were wholly ignorant of the matter. —Have I not, Flora?"

" Yes, my dear brother," replied Flora, blushing; " and I also tried to convince mamma that Edward was ignorant of it, from his manner of beseeching that I would immediately endeavour to find Miss Lindsay, and to communicate to her the letter of her father."

" Thank you—thank you, my lovely friend!" said Edward, pressing her hand to his lips—" you only did me justice; yet,

had

had either your brother or Miss Lindsay thought proper to have made me their confidant, although I would have tried to persuade them to give up so rash, so ill-judged a step, yet I should also have felt myself in honour bound not to betray them."

" Ah, do not tell that to my mother!" cried Flora, with a look of beseeching earnestness; " say any thing rather than that you would not have apprised her of my brother's elopement, had you known it."

" Dearly as I value the good opinion of lady Manningham," replied Edward, " I would not purchase it by the sacrifice of my integrity. Nothing would tempt me to betray any confidence which might be reposed in me."

" Then she will continue to think you privy to their flight," said Flora, mournfully, " in spite of all our endeavours to persuade her to the contrary."

" How," cried Edward, warmly, at the

same moment letting fall the hand of Flora, " will her ladyship doubt my word? will she disbelieve my positive assertion that I had no concern in the elopement of her son?"

" No, certainly, I meant not—But you are angry with me, Mr. Mackenzie," said Flora, in a trembling voice.

" Oh, not with you, dearest, kindest Flora!" exclaimed Edward, retaking her hand; " to be angry with *you* would be impossible."

" Almost impossible," said Frederic; " and yet both my father and mother have been a little offended at our defending you so warmly, Mackenzie."

A loud knocking at the door called the attention of Frederic to the window.— " It is them," said he; " and with them comes lord George and his sister. Constantia, I suppose, remains with sir Arthur and his mother."

At the mention of lord George's name, Edward became for a moment pale. He

cast

cast an inquiring glance towards Flora, who, disconcerted, and evidently uneasy, said—" I wish they had staid away: I was in hopes we should have been alone to-day."

Edward felt revived.—" If she loved him," thought he, " she would not wish for his absence."

The door now opened, and sir Charles and lady Manningham entered. Not as usual did they greet with friendly smiles the presence of Edward—not as usual did they extend their hands towards him, as a token of kindness and of welcome. Yet they seemed pleased once more to behold him at their house, although their notice of him was slight and distant. Lady Manningham desired Flora to get ready to accompany lord George and his sister, who had come purposely to give her an airing in Hyde-Park.

Flora evidently obeyed with reluctance; and in a few minutes Edward found himself alone with her parents and Frederic,

not

not however without having first encountered the strict investigation of lady Jane's
eyes, who gave him to understand that
she thought him an object worthy of her
attention.

"We have not seen you, Mr. Mackenzie, since the night of the ball," said lady
Manningham, coldly. "You have not
been accustomed to let so long a period
elapse between your visits."

"Your ladyship will have the goodness
to remember," said Edward, respectfully,
"that until now I have never had so
painful an occasion to command my absence."

"Do you mean the death of Mrs. Lindsay, or the shameful elopement of her
daughter?" inquired lady Manningham,
looking steadily in his face.

"I might say both," replied Edward,
"since the unfortunate circumstance of
Miss Lindsay's imprudent flight has so
deeply affected her father, that but for our
intended

intended journey to-morrow, I should still
have been debarred the pleasure of seeing
your ladyship."

" If I thought that Mr. Lindsay was
ignorant of his daughter's attachment to
my son," said sir Charles, " or, of what
is of most consequence, their premeditated
elopement, I should feel most sensibly for
his situation; but I can hardly believe it
possible that a young woman, reared with
such doting fondness as Miss Lindsay
was, should conceal from her parents a
circumstance on which the whole happiness of her life depended."

" I think that I may venture to affirm,"
replied Edward, " that neither Mr. nor
Mrs. Lindsay for a moment suspected what
has happened. Indeed, when you reflect,
sir Charles, upon Miss Lindsay's supposed
engagement to Mr. Vivian, you will be
convinced that her parents would never
sanction so cruel a breach of faith. Nay,
I am inclined to believe that neither Mr.
Manningham nor Clara had determined

E 3 upon

upon their flight an hour before it took place."

" Were not *you* the confidant of their shameless disregard to decency and public opinion?" inquired lady Manningham, with a look of scrutinizing attention.

" Chance informed me of their intention to elope," replied Edward, " but I had not the power to prevent its taking place."

" And what prevented your informing me of a circumstance of so much importance?" said lady Manningham. "I might surely have expected from you, Mr. Mackenzie, a far different conduct. You confess that you knew that my eldest son, and the proud hope of his family, was on the point of disgracing himself for ever, and yet you suffered him to run blindly to his ruin, without once attempting to save him or his relations from unavoidable misery."

" I have already mentioned to your ladyship," replied Edward, " that to chance alone I was indebted for my knowledge of

Mr.

Mr. Manningham's new-formed plans. In-disposition obliged me to retire to a private apartment, to which I was conducted by Frederic, who had scarcely left me to repose for a few minutes on a couch, when Mr. Manningham and Miss Lindsay entered the chamber. They were too much occupied by their own feelings to cast a glance towards that part of the room where I was, and I thus, most painfully for myself, became unwillingly acquainted with the cause of their mutual recriminations. They ended in an agreement to elope immediately. Mr. Manningham left the apartment to give orders for a chaise to be procured; and so completely was I overcome by grief, vexation, and horror, at the idea of what the dying mother of Clara must suffer if the elopement took place, that I could not repress a groan which then escaped me, and which alarmed Miss Lindsay. It was in vain that I besought her to delay her union—in vain that I conjured her to think before she determined upon

an

an act which would bring with it its own severe punishment. All my persuasions were unavailing: she left me in haste, and though I followed almost instantly, she eluded all my vigilance. The note which I received shortly after from her father called for my immediate presence at home; but I left a message to be delivered to Miss Lindsay, which I hoped would hasten her return, and prevent her rash and imprudent journey."

" That is putting the mildest construction on the case," said sir Charles; " this last unfeeling act of levity has convinced me of what I before suspected, that Miss Lindsay is selfish, cold-hearted, and undutiful: she is therefore the last woman on earth that I should have expected Charles to make choice of for a wife. It however affords me great satisfaction, Edward, to learn from yourself that you were not privy to their transgression; for it would have been a sad mortification both to me and lady Manningham, to have
                              found

found that you; whom we so sincerely regard and esteem, were a party in an affair
which so materially affects our peace."

" It gives me equal pleasure to hear
the same," replied lady Manningham; "yet
I cannot help regretting that Edward had
neither time nor opportunity to communicate to us what he had overheard: we
might then have taken proper precautions
to prevent their elopement."

Edward was silent; but sir Charles,
rising hastily from his seat, said, in an
angry tone—" Cease to regret what is now
past cure, my dear Constantia. Charles
has made his own election, at the risk of
our eternal displeasure; but as I feel too
painfully assured of what will be his future unhappiness, when reason and reflection regain their influence over his mind,
I shall not add to his self-upbraidings by
my reproaches or my resentment."

Sir Charles now quitted the chamber;
and lady Manningham, sighing deeply at
the probable misery of a darling son, now

turned

·rned towards Edward with all her usual·
·omplacency, and asked him some ques-·
tions relative to his intended journey, and
his afflicted companion.

Edward, highly·as he esteemed her
ladyship, chose, from·motives of delicacy,
to conceal the embarrassed state of·Mr.·
Lindsay's affairs, and·yet he felt himself·
in a manner compelled to avow the cause
of their sudden departure·from London,
lest she should be offended at his seeming
want of·confidence.

·Lady Manningham now for the·first·
time expressed·some friendly concern for·
the desolate condition·of Mr. Lindsay.—
" I pity him sincerely," said·she; " for·to
have only one child, and that·child·so
worthless, so cruel, so unnatural, is indeed
to be most sorely afflicted. Never shall I
be able to·look again on Clara Lindsay·
without a shudder of'horror, as I reflect
upon the doting fondness of her poor
mother, and the sad, sad return she met
with from·her unfeeling daughter.·The
only

only consolation now left for her deserted parent must flow from your affection and tender attentions. Poor Mr. Lindsay! tell him, Edward, that I would have called on him to-morrow, but for his intended journey."

Lady Manningham now proceeded to inform Edward, that she had that morning heard from lady James Osborne, who had enclosed tickets for a ball, which was fixed for the last day of that month.—" Her ladyship has requested me to forward one to you," said lady Manningham, "and I therefore hope that, if possible, you will endeavour to be in town time enough to avail yourself of her invitation."

Edward replied, that he should be extremely happy to accept of her ladyship's kindness; but as it was particular business that called for his presence at ——, the day of his return was uncertain; he would, however, try, if possible, to be in town in time to attend at lady James's.

" Her ladyship also communicated to

me

me a piece of intelligence," said lady Manningham, " which, I fear, will not afford you equal satisfaction. The marchioness of Anendale has lost her son; we may therefore expect soon to see her return to England announced in the public papers."

Edward, although he anticipated this event, could not help feeling extremely shocked, now that it was mentioned to him as having taken place. · Never had he felt before so warm an interest in the fate of so young a child—never had he experienced more pain than that which he now did, on being assured that the interesting form of the young earl would no more gladden his sight in this world. Perhaps, also, the death of his little friend brought to his remembrance his beautiful mother, and the deep affliction which at that moment she must be suffering. " Can *she* feel a mother's pangs?" thought Edward — " *she* who could so coldly counsel another to abandon her helpless offspring? Oh! if at this hour her heart is bursting at the loss of her darling

ling son—if at this moment it swells with
all a mother's tenderest, softest, dearest feelings—all-righteous Heaven! remind her
of the terrible sacrifice which, in the days
of her early years, she would have imposed
upon the parent who gave me being!"

Edward's heart insensibly softened towards the marchioness, as his mind dwelt
with lingering sadness on her supposed
grief; and, had he not been ashamed of his
own weakness, he would fain have endeavoured to palliate a crime at which his
heart sickened, and his nature revolted.
Fortunately for Edward, the situation of
Mr. Lindsay, and the embarrassment of
his affairs, drew off his attention from the
dangerous contemplation of what his ardent
fancy had pictured to be the state of lady
Anendale. The melancholy despondency
of poor Mr. Lindsay soon left Edward no
time to brood over fancied sorrows; even
the marchioness, her beauty, her faults, and
her maternal agonies, were forgotten by
Edward, as he found himself called upon

to

to make every exertion to rouse the languid spirits of his early patron, and to call off his thoughts from the ungrateful desertion of his only child.

## CHAPTER V.

THE return of Edward and Mr. Lindsay, at so dull a season of the year, created no small surprise among the inhabitants of the little village of ———. Various conjectures went abroad respecting it, as well as remarks on the hasty and ill-timed marriage of Miss Lindsay with young squire Manningham; but all agreed in censuring Clara for her sad want of filial affection, as well as common humanity, in abandoning her tender mother on the eve of her dissolution.

Sally, though by no means a faultless character herself, was equally shocked by the

the dreadful levity displayed by her young mistress, as well as piqued at her being kept in ignorance of her intended flight. This last feeling made a convert of Sally, and she therefore scrupled not to confess to William Ashford and his wife all the mean and malignant schemes of her lady to injure Patty, and to rouse the jealousy of her husband, which she hoped would be the means of breaking off all friendly intimacy between him and Edward Mackenzie. The generous soul of Ashford immediately acknowledged its error, and resolved upon a speedy atonement, by avowing, both to Sally and his wife, the secret influence which the communications of the former had had upon his mind, at the same time that he determined to conduct himself in future towards Edward, in a manner which should convince him that he was both ready and willing to acknowledge that he had done him injustice.

Edward was therefore most pleasingly surprised, when he called to inquire after
the

the health of Patty, to hear himself addressed by her husband in terms the most respectful, and to find himself actually pressed to await her return by Ashford, who before had treated him with so repelling a coldness, that Edward had almost resolved never again to enter his house. Affection for Patty, joined to the persuasions of honest Oliver, had overcome the scruples of Edward, and he, therefore, took the first opportunity of Mr. Lindsay's being engaged with Mr. Curwen, Edward's kind preceptor, who had come to pass the evening with him, to make a short visit to Mrs. Ashford.

If Edward was agreeably disappointed in the reception which he met with from Ashford, how was the satisfaction which he felt increased when, at the return of Patty, he solicited, as an honour, that he would stand godfather to their little boy, whose name it was already decided should be that of Patty's first and dearest friend. Edward caught the infant from the fond

arms

arms of his mother, and smothering him
with kisses, promised not only to become
his godfather, but to keep in view his future interests and future happiness as sacredly as if he were his own. It is need-
less to observe the heartfelt delight of
Patty upon this occasion, as she knew Edward too well not to be assured that his
promise was not the promise of the moment, but one that came from his heart,
one that would be faithfully and rigidly
performed.

Edward now found himself called upon
to act and to think with a judgment far
beyond either his years or experience.
Mr. Lindsay's despondency continued to
increase to an alarming degree, and to render him wholly incapable of assisting in
the arrangement of his affairs. In this
painful exigency, Edward with gratitude
accepted of the kind aid of Mr. Curwen,
who afforded him the most prompt and
friendly support in the complicated business of Mr. Lindsay's concerns, and who,
with

with equal kindness, persuaded the afflicted parent to take up his residence with
him, as all the furniture and effects were
to be disposed of to defray his debts. Mr.
Lindsay yielded to the persuasions of Edward, and retired to the hospitable abode
of Mr. Curwen, while Edward and honest
Oliver remained to execute the trust reposed in them.

At the death of old Margaret Grey, Mr.
Lindsay had ordered what little property
she died possessed of to be removed to his
house, where it had remained ever since,
and where Edward now discovered it,
carefully locked up in a spare room, of
which Mr. Lindsay had kept the key. He
could not behold, without some degree of
emotion, the various articles which had
been so familiar to him in the days of his
happy childhood. They recalled to his
memory the kind endearing old woman
to whom they had formerly belonged, and
with her remembrance was blended that of
his young and innocent companion, Patty
Smith.

Smith. To him the effects of his venerable grandmother were useless, but to her they might be of service; and who so well deserved to possess them as the tender and gentle nurse of Margaret Grey? Oliver was therefore commissioned to remove what Edward had long considered to be his own property to the house of William Ashford, while he hastened before him to apprise Patty of his intended gift.

Had Edward presented Mrs. Ashford with the most costly furniture for her abode, it could not have been received with more grateful delight than that which she now expressed on again beholding the well-known articles, which habit and circumstances had rendered dear to her. With pride and exultation she placed the high-backed chair of her revered schoolmistress in its former station, declaring that she would never resign its ease and comfort to any one, except sometimes to her husband, as a great indulgence, or to Edward, whenever he condescended to honour them

by

by his presence; then, and only then, would Patty give up the sacred seat of her dear old friend.

- When the distressing business of the sale was over, poor Mr. Lindsay found himself dispossessed of every thing which had once constituted his pride and pleasure. From feelings which did honour to his principles, he gave up to his creditors even the jewels of his wife, remarking that justice demanded of him this sacrifice, and that his ungrateful child must resign her claim to those who could assert a stronger, since the chief of his embarrassments had arisen from her selfish extravagance. This painful duty performed, he again relapsed into his melancholy state of apparent insensibility, from which nothing could rouse him but the voice of Edward, or the genuine tears of pity which Oliver would frequently shed over his unhappy master. Thinking that a change of scene, joined to the tender assiduities of Mrs. Alexander Mackenzie, might alleviate his silent and uncomplaining

uncomplaining grief, Edward prepared to return to London the day after he had stood godfather to Patty's infant son.

Mr. Curwen, at whose house Edward and Mr. Lindsay still remained, gave to his senior pupils a dinner, to which all the old schoolfellows of Mackenzie were invited, that they might again meet together and talk over their boyish exploits. That the young men might not feel either their conversation or their hilarity restrained by the presence of their preceptor, Mr. Curwen and his melancholy guest retired early from the dinner-table to a distant apartment, leaving orders with the attendant servants to supply all the wants of his gay and happy pupils. Wit, good-humour, and the pleasing recollection of past events, contributed to circulate the glass with greater freedom than prudence warranted, and Edward, for the first time in his life, felt the dangerous intoxication of the senses, as he rose to accompany some of his companions home, whom he considered

considered in a more helpless state than himself.

With a feverish pulse, an aching head, and unsteady feet, Edward found himself alone at the gate of Ashford's house. It was late, and the man was shutting up the shop when Edward inquired, in a voice not perfectly audible, if his master was at home?

" No, sir, master is gone to the club, and won't be home till late; but mistress is in the parlour, if you'll please to walk in."

Edward staggered into the room where Patty was sitting, and throwing himself into a chair, leaned his head against the wall, while Patty, alarmed, hastily placed her sleeping infant in the cradle, and then advancing towards him, inquired if he was unwell. His look and manner betrayed the cause of his indisposition; she therefore persuaded him to take possession of the high-backed chair of his grandmother, while she procured him some strong coffee, which in a great degree restored him to a

knowledge

knowledge of what was passing. Edward's head became clearer, but the influence of the wine still remained, and saddened his feelings. Patty's spirits were that evening none of the highest; she had seen her father in the course of the day, and learnt from him that he was on the brink of ruin, to which his own follies, and the increasing extravagance of his housekeeper, had at last brought him, and he confessed that he had nothing before him but the prospect of a jail, unless he could raise by the next morning the sum of twenty pounds to pay part of a debt of sixty. Ashford had refused to advance him the money, or even to assist him in any way, unless he gave up for ever all future intimacy with his profligate companion. This proposal was rejected by Mr. Smith; and Patty was weeping over the probable fate of her infatuated father, when Edward, by his unexpected presence, called off her attention to himself.

Patty had, from a little girl, been in the habit

habit of confiding to Edward all that con-
cerned herself and her family, as far in the
latter case as her delicacy would allow; and
now that she saw him tolerably composed
and rational, she felt her mind relieved in
pouring forth to him as usual the present
grief which oppressed her. Patty had been
sadly neglected by her father, and sometimes had been treated harshly by him;
but neither his neglect nor his occasional
severity had weakened her sense of filial
duty, or lessened her filial tenderness: her
father was unhappy—his liberty was endangered, his property exhausted, and his
only prospect a prison; could, therefore,
a daughter's heart feel light, while that
of an only parent was bursting with the
pressure of misfortunes, no matter whether
unmerited or deserved?

All the money that Edward was at present master of did not amount to more
than twelve pounds; this he instantly tendered to Mrs. Ashford with an air of
joyous satisfaction, congratulating himself
that

that he possessed the means to assist her in her present hour of difficulty and distress; yet regretting that the sum was not adequate to the wants of her father.

Patty's eyes filled with grateful tears at this proof of generous friendship; but as she was wholly unable to raise the remaining eight pounds, and as twenty was the least that her father's creditor would accept, she declined receiving the assistance of Edward, unwilling to inconvenience him by taking what would not relieve her father.

" I thank you a thousand times over, dear Mr. Edward," said Patty, " but I will not take the twelve pounds, since it is wholly out of my power to procure the rest of the money, as I have not a shilling that William does not know of. Thank you all the same for your goodness, but my poor father must go to prison—I know he must."

" He shall not go, Patty," cried Edward warmly, " he shall not go to pri-

son! For your sake I will endeavour to
raise the remaining eight pounds. Mr.
Curwen, I dare say, will lend me that sum,
if I leave in his hands my watch as a security."

"What, part with your watch!" exclaimed Patty, in amazement—"the watch
which your dear father Mackenzie gave
you, and which you value as highly as you
do your life! Oh no, Mr. Edward, no;
I cannot think of your making so great a
sacrifice for my sake."

"That, and a still greater sacrifice, beloved Patty, would I make to purchase
your ease and happiness," said Edward,
throwing his arms tenderly round the
weeping Patty, and pressing his lips to her
crimson cheek. "Who in this wide world
can bring forward a stronger claim upon
my affection than yourself?—who loves
me so firmly, so faithfully, as you do, Patty? Have we not been brought up together under this dear though humble roof?
and were not the last, almost the last words

of

of our revered preceptress, that we should continue to love each other through life? In this at least we have obeyed my grandmother—have we not, Patty?"

"Oh, Mr. Edward," sobbed Patty, "why do you remind me of those innocent and happy days, when ignorant of the distinctions of birth and fortune, my only aim. was to please and to fulfil your wishes—my only hope to be rewarded by your praise? If my heart too faithfully obeyed the exhortations of my revered friend, and prized too warmly your approbation, instead of that of my near relations, the fault is not my own. Habit made your opinion dear to me—habit made your presence, *at one time*, almost necessary to my existence. For your sake I braved the malice of Miss Lindsay, the insolence of Mr. Manningham, and I was nearly ready to brave the anger of my father, sooner than consent to give up your friendship. My father forbade me to speak to you again; but though I was loth to disobey *him* who

gave

gave me being, yet, if he had turned me into the streets, without a home or without a friend, my heart told me that it would break before it could ever cease to feel for you the kind sentiments of my childhood."

Edward pressed the affectionate Patty to his breast with a warmth and energy of feeling which recalled the wandering thoughts of Mrs. Ashford. She gently disengaged herself from his embrace, and looking modestly, yet steadily, in his glowing face, she said—" I would not have confessed to any one but yourself, Mr. Edward, the nature and strength of my attachment; but *you* will never cause me to repent my unguarded candour. I am no longer at liberty to dwell with delight on the scenes of my early days, no longer mistress of my own actions; gratitude and esteem made me become the wife of Ashford, and affection now binds me to the father of my child: but when you offered to part with so dear a treasure as the parting gift of serjeant Mackenzie, and

and to part with it on my account, I could not keep my feelings within proper bounds."

Edward felt in a' moment the impropriety of his conduct, and immediately became sober. He pressed the hand of Patty to his lips with respectful tenderness— " Beloved Patty! beloved sister!" he exclaimed, " it is the first, and it shall be the last time that you will ever have cause to lament my having yielded to intemperance. I am no longer under the dangerous influence of intoxication—I am myself again, Patty, and the same friend, brother, and companion, that you knew in your childhood. It was here, in this well-remembered room, that our first affections burst forth—it was here that they were nurtured and cherished by my sainted grandmother—and it was also here that I saw, for the last time, the best, the dearest, and the noblest of men. From his hands I received this precious gift," continued Edward, drawing forth his watch, " and

gave

gave a promise never to part with it, unless to save the life of a fellow-creature.
In snatching your father, Patty, from the
horrors of a prison, I shall perform an action of equal magnitude—I shall dry your
tears, my faithful friend, and perhaps preserve the peace of your future years, which
would be endangered should any thing
unpleasant happen to your father.   Trust,
therefore, to my endeavours, Patty, to relieve your father, and do not grieve at the
means by which he will be succoured.
My watch will remain safe with Mr. Curwen, until I can repay the money, and that
will be in the course of a few weeks."

Patty's feelings were too much awakened to be checked without extreme difficulty, and Edward, rising hastily from his
chair, would have quitted her that she
might give way to them freely ; but Patty,
placing her hand on his arm, could not
suffer him to depart without pouring forth
a part of her gratitude before him.   Edward promised to send Oliver early the
next

next morning to her with the remainder of the money, that she might be in time to convey it to her father by the hour appointed by his remorseless creditor.

" I know not when I shall see you, or hear from you again," said Patty, still holding his arm, " but my blessings will follow you ever. I shall think of you, Mr. Edward, I shall pray for you, and trust in the goodness of Heaven to guard and save you from the dangerous intimacy of the marchioness of Anendale."

" The recollection of her heartless counsel to my mother will shield me from the power of her enchantments," replied Edward. "If we should ever meet again, she will have lost her influence over my soul and senses."

" I hope so, I hope so, Mr. Edward," exclaimed Patty, fervently; " for I dread the thought of your getting into her power, as much as if her very look and breath were poisonous. Be sure, dear Mr. Edward, when you see the marchioness, to

F 4 think

think of your grandmother's words—' An angel's form and a devil's heart.' Oh, I can never forget them !''

Edward promised to remember them as often as Patty could possibly wish; then assuring her that he should expect to hear either from her or her husband, as often as they had leisure, concerning the health of his little godson, he reluctantly left Mrs. Ashford, and hurried back to Mr. Curwen's, where, fortunately for his wishes, he found that gentleman waiting supper for him alone, as Mr. Lindsay had retired to his chamber for the night.

Edward, with some embarrassment, made his wants known to Mr. Curwen, requesting him to oblige him with the loan of eight pounds, and offering to deposit his watch in his hands until he should be able to repay the money. Mr. Curwen listened to his young favourite with great attention, as well as considerable surprise. He knew that in the course of the day he had seen him with several bank-notes, and

he

he therefore wondered the more at his present request, as he thought it impossible that in the course of a few hours he could be pennyless. He resolved, nevertheless, to grant his wish, at the same time that he could not avoid being desirous to learn the cause which had occasioned Edward to make it.

Mr. Curwen took out his pocket-book, and, counting out the notes, said—" There, Edward, is what you asked me for—but had you not better take ten of them? You may not receive your money as soon as you expect, and it will be awkward for you to be without a guinea, in case you want one."

Edward most gratefully accepted the kind offer of Mr. Curwen, presenting him at the same time his highly-treasured watch, and promising to redeem it as early as possible.

" No," said Mr. Curwen, " no, Edward, I will not deprive you of so necessary a companion. I know you too well, my dear

boy,

boy, to require any other security than your word—that is sufficient; pay me when you can, but do not distress yourself. And now, my dear young friend, think not that any idle or impertinent curiosity prompts me to pry into your affairs, but think that it is my fatherly anxiety for your welfare and happiness that makes me wish to learn by what means it became necessary that you should apply to me for eight pounds, when this morning you were yourself master of nearly twice that sum. I flatter myself, Edward, that I have proved myself worthy to be trusted by you; and if the nature of your demand will permit explanation, confide to me the cause. I pass my word never to let it escape my lips, be it what it may."

Edward felt that he could make a confidant of Mr. Curwen, and he therefore scrupled not to acknowledge the occasion for which the money was borrowed, adding, that he hoped Mr. Smith would take warning from his present misfortunes, and repent

repent of his past conduct before he was completely ruined.

Mr. Curwen shook his head emphatically—" I am grieved, my dear boy," said he, " to find that your benevolence has been thrown away upon a worthlesss object, and the more so, as twenty pounds is a sum of consequence to so young a man as yourself, as well as a sum that might have been so much better disposed of, had you bestowed it otherwise. As it is, I consider it as lost to you for ever. Smith has no principle, no remains of honesty or of honour; he will receive your money, but he will never think of repaying you."

" But if, by saving him from the walls of a prison," replied Edward, " I have also saved his amiable daughter from the severest pang which her filial affection could experience, I have more than repaid myself for the loss of my money, and I even rejoice that an opportunity has occurred to enable me to discharge a part of my debt of gratitude to Mrs. Ashford, for her

kind

kind and uniform tenderness to my grandmother, during her last severe illness."

Mr. Curwen took the hand of Edward,
and pressed it within his own—" Blest age
of pure and innocent enthusiasm!" said
he, " when the best and noblest affections
of our nature are so keenly alive to the
call of gratitude or honour! Oh! wherefore should a more intimate connexion
with the world repress the generous
warmth of youthful feelings, and teach us
the sad lesson that dissimulation and dis-
guise are necessary! Such, however, is the
case, my dear Edward; therefore, as a
friend I warn you, as a father I advise you,
to check the grateful overflowings of your
heart, lest you should injure both the
character and the peace of her whose happiness you have thus kindly, thus disin-
terestedly consulted. You need not blush,
my son, for well can I enter into the nature of your sentiments towards Mrs. Ashford—well can I appreciate the state of
your feelings for each other, brought up
together

together under the same roof, and tutored
for a time by the same worthy and excel-
lent being, whose chief aim perhaps was to
increase and strengthen the tenderness of
your childhood's friendship. But, my dear
Edward, the love which then was guileless
might now become otherwise. Patty is
no longer the girlish companion of your
boyhood—she is no longer free to devote
her time and thoughts to any other than
her husband. He it is who must now constitute her earthly happiness—he it is who
ought solely to fill both her heart and her
mind, while you must now be content to
occupy only a secondary place in each. I
regret to say, that such is the state of
things in this world, Edward, that were it
to be known from whence Smith received
his present assistance, the character of Mrs.
Ashford might suffer so severe a wound,
that her future peace would be considerably endangered. I mention this, my dear
young friend, merely to caution you
against too openly giving way to your
kindness

kindness for your early companion, not from the remotest suspicion, on my part, that in any other respect such caution is necessary."

Edward thanked Mr. Curwen for his paternal counsels, assuring him that he would not fail to remember them, and to regulate his future conduct according to his friendly advice. They then parted for the night, Edward feeling but too conscious of the justness of Mr. Curwen's ideas of propriety, from his own unguarded freedom of behaviour that evening; and Mr. Curwen, though ignorant of that behaviour, was nevertheless sensible of the probable danger of a connexion between two young people attached to each other from infancy, and linked together by a reciprocity of kind and mutual obligations. He therefore felt some degree of satisfaction in knowing that Edward's speedy removal to London would place him out of the reach of the evil which he dreaded, and at the same time preserve the character of Mrs Ashford

Ashford from the poisonous breath of village slander.

## CHAPTER VI.

EDWARD was up by break of day. It had been his first intention to dispatch Oliver with a letter to Mrs. Ashford, but the reflections of the night suggested that this mode of conveying the money to Patty was both dangerous and imprudent. He therefore dressed himself with quickness, resolving to call and take leave of her husband, and trust to chance for an opportunity to slip into the hands of Mrs. Ashford the sum which was necessary to procure the lenity of her father's creditor.

Chance did favour the wishes of Edward, who hastened to the house of Ashford, just at the moment when he was busily engaged in his morning's usual occupation.

pation.   He passed into the parlour, where
Patty received, with some degree of confusion, the promised relief; but Edward
staid not to hear her thanks; pressing
her hand, he motioned her to be silent,
then kissing the cheek of his little name-
sake, he left the room, and after shaking
its honest father most cordially by the
hand, and wishing him and his family all
imaginable good fortune, Edward as hastily returned to Mr. Curwen, to whom he
secretly imparted the cause of his morning's walk, and then joined Mr. Lindsay,
who received him with a melancholy smile,
telling him that he was ready to begin his
journey immediately after breakfast.

" During our absence yesterday from
the dining-parlour, my dear Edward," said
Mr. Lindsay, " I was occupied in writing
to my uncle, who is in Ireland, and who
holds considerable property in that king-
dom.   This I was induced to by the kind
advice of Mr. Curwen, who has indeed interested himself as warmly in my concerns

as

as if he were my brother; to have rejected his counsels would have been ungrateful: yet why should I seek to mix
again with a world of which I am so sadly
weary?—why wish to prolong an existence made wretched to me by the heartless conduct of my only child?"

" While the world contains one heart
devotedly attached to you, my dear sir,"
replied Edward affectionately, " your existence ought to be deemed valuable; and
I flatter myself that you have not yet to
learn that there are more hearts than one,
on whose fidelity and kindness you may
with safety rely."

" Ah, Edward !" said the afflicted father
of Clara, " I acknowledge, with humble
gratitude, the mercy of my Creator—I feel
his goodness every hour that I hear your
voice; yet, as I bend beneath his will, my
paternal feelings rise up against my sub-
missive inclinations, and as I think of my
unfeeling daughter, I wish that I no longer lived, that I no longer continued to
breathe

breathe the same vital air as that which she inhales. Prodigal in my love, lavish in my tenderness, I weakly trusted to the filial duty of my child, as the staff of my declining years; but she has abandoned me in one of the most painful trials of my life—she has left me to struggle with my misfortunes, uncheered by her smiles, unassisted by her attentions; she has forsaken in her last moments the parent who gave her being, and the chain is broken for ever that bound her to the fond confiding heart of her father."

" Mrs. Manningham will plead her own cause," said Edward, " as soon as she returns. A repentant daughter cannot sue in vain, if she appeals to the tender feelings of so kind a parent."

" No future penitence can expiate her crime in my eyes," replied Mr. Lindsay, sternly. " She who could forsake the deathbed of one of the tenderest, best of mothers, who could think of selfish pleasures while the expiring breath trembled

on

on that mother's lip; she who could do this must not dare to insult the sacredness of a father's griefs by any vain and fruitless shew of late repentance. My heart disclaims the worthless idol which it so long has worshipped; and should she venture through your means to intrude herself upon my notice, I demand it as a favour, Edward—nay, as the strongest proof of your regard, that you will not suffer her to approach my presence, that you will not receive any letters which her matchless effrontery may induce her to convey to you; for never again, while I exist, will I hold the slightest communication with her who was *once* my daughter."

Edward felt too much respect for the wounded affection of Mr. Lindsay to attempt at this moment to soften his resentment towards his child. He assured him that, far from doing any thing which could add to his distress of mind, it would be his study to lighten it as much as possible, and that he hoped, that for *his* sake, he

would

would not allow his endeavours to prove fruitless.

Mr. Lindsay tenderly embraced his kind young friend, who now left him to inquire of Oliver if every thing was ready for their departure.

Mrs. Alexander Mackenzie had expected them; therefore, when the travellers arrived, they were greeted with the smiles of true benevolence and respectful hospitality, which were not the less welcome to the afflicted mind of Mr. Lindsay, because they came from one whom fortune had placed in a sphere of life inferior to his own. Mary Mackenzie heaped fresh faggots on the drawing-room fire, re-swept the hearth, and modestly inquired if she should pour out their coffee, while her mother was busily engaged in toasting the muffins?

Mr. Lindsay, to whom every shew of kindness was now of double value, readily accepted of the offer, though it was not without a great deal of entreaty and persuasion

suasion that he could prevail upon Mary to sit in his presence.

When a little recovered from the fatigues of his journey, Mr. Lindsay reminded Edward that this was the evening fixed on by lady James Osborne for her public night, and assured him, that unless he honoured her ticket, he should feel considerably disappointed.—" To tell you the truth, Edward," said he, " I recollected your invitation, and it made me anxious to be in town to-day : but for that, I should not have left my friend Curwen this week ; therefore go you must. I shall do extremely well, as Mrs. Mackenzie and her daughter Mary have promised to be my companions until bed-time."

Thus assured that Mr. Lindsay would not be left to his own melancholy reflections, Edward consented to quit him, confident that both Mrs. Alexander Mackenzie and Mary would do their utmost to make him comfortable and happy.

It may not here be unnecessary to observe,

serve, that although the former was compelled, at the death of her husband, to
open a fruiterer's shop for the support of
her family, yet it was one of the better
sort, and celebrated for the finest articles
of the kind.  She had now lived twenty
years in the same house, and had brought
up her children with credit and respecta-
bility, giving them all good plain educa-
tions, and placing them in different trades,
which enabled them to support themselves.  Mary, more delicate, and more
handsome than the other girls, remained
at home with her mother, whom she as-
sisted in her business, filling up her leisure hours by needlework, which she procured from the ladies who frequently called on her mother to order their own fruit.
Mary was engaged to a young man in the
employment of a person who kept a large
bookseller's shop at the court end of the
town, and to whom she was to be married
in a few months.

Her person, her manners, and her disposition,

position, were highly engaging; Edward therefore felt little doubt but that Mr. Lindsay would pass his evening agreeably, and he prepared to fulfil his engagement to lady James, not without the pleasing hope that he might be a successful candidate for the dear hand of Flora Manningham.

Oliver was dispatched for a coach; and Edward, when he had finished dressing, returned to where Mr. Lindsay and Mrs. Alexander Mackenzie were sitting.

" God bless you for an ornament to the name of Mackenzie!" said she, warmly. " Oh that my poor brother-in-law could but see you now! how his brave heart would exult in the child of its adoption! —I forgot, Mr. Edward, to tell you that Miss Manningham was married last week to sir Arthur Vivian; I saw it in the Sunday-paper; and I hope I shall live to see the day when your marriage with some great lady will be announced in the same way.—You will pardon me, sir," continued she,

she, turning towards Mr. Lindsay, " for the freedom of my speech, but Mr. Edward Mackenzie is almost as dear to me as one of my own sons. He was not two months old when I first saw him, and had his mother allowed me, I would' have suckled him myself with my own baby. I lost sight of him too soon, but I have never forgotten him, and I said then, and I still say the same, that I am sure that he is born to be a great man."

" I will trust to your prophecy, my dear friend," replied Edward, " though I confess that it would puzzle me to tell from whence my greatness is to come."

" Some day or other you will find out who was your father," said Mrs. Alexander, " as well as for what purpose so strange a mark as that of a coronet was placed on your arm. But here comes the coach. Oh that I was able to follow you unseen, to hear all the fine things that will be said of you this evening. Many a great lady will

will cast a look and heave a sigh for Mr. Edward Mackenzie."

"You must not try to make my young favourite vain," said Mr. Lindsay, " or you will rob him of one of his best qualities."

Edward affectionately pressed their hands, while the smile of grateful pleasure beamed on each handsome feature of his face. It was the smile that so often enchanted honest Oliver, who now stood with the door half open, admiring the appearance of the being whom he loved dearest in the world, and whom to be separated from, he felt would be far worse than poverty or death.

The Miss Osbornes were the first who caught the name of Edward, as the servant announced his arrival, and immediately came forward to receive him with familiar and undisguised pleasure.—" This is an unexpected happiness, Mr. Mackenzie," cried Maria, gaily; " mamma had given you up. I would inquire after your

health, but that I see it is quite unnecessary.   When did you come to town?"

Upon Edward's replying only that evening—"Well," added she, "then we are
the more obliged to you for remembering
that this is our public night.   But let me
lead you to mamma; she is actually impatient to present you to my uncle Richard."

The satisfaction which instantly became
visible in the countenance of lady James
was extremely gratifying to the feelings
of Edward.   She not only held out her
hand, but made room for him between
herself and a gentleman, to whom she instantly introduced Edward, with a warmth
and eagerness of manner that convinced
him that he had been the subject of their
private conversation.

Lady James, then turning towards Edward, inquired in the kindest accents after
his welfare, assuring him that she felt herself highly flattered by his readiness to
oblige her by his presence, when he must
necessarily be fatigued by his journey.

" Mr.

" Mr. Mackenzie is of an age to think lightly of fatigue, my dear sister," said Mr. Colvill. " The effects of travelling will soon be forgotten, when he has selected from among the beauties of the ball-room some favourite fair to be his partner in the dance. When I was his age——"

A deep sigh left the sentence unfinished.

" Ah, my beloved Richard !" exclaimed lady James, in a voice of tenderness, " well do I remember that at Mr. Mackenzie's age you were the most animated, the most happy, but the most romantic creature in the world. You were the life, the joy of your family and friends. You were, in fact, every thing that Mr. Mackenzie now is. I shall not rest till my father has seen you, Mr. Mackenzie—until he tells me that you are the living image of what my brother was at your age."

" Still the same warm-hearted being as when a girl," said Mr. Colvill, forcing a smile, as he pressed the hand of lady James. " Do you know, Mr. Mackenzie, that this

dear

dear sister of mine has actually been so
nervously impatient for your return to
town, that I seriously became uneasy lest
it should affect her health. When you
learn how firmly we have been attached
from our infancy, you will cease to wonder at the warmth of her feelings towards
yourself, who, as she compliments me
by saying, bear a resemblance to what I
was when I left England."

Edward replied, that from whatever
cause the kindness of lady James origi-
nated, he should deem himself as singu-
larly fortunate in being its object, and that
he hoped her ladyship would not think
him too presuming if he said that his
heart felt disposed to return that flattering kindness by every mark of gratitude
and respect.

The exhilarating sounds of a fine band
of music made Edward turn his head me-
chanically towards the ball-room.

Olivia Osborne stood near him; he inquired if she was disengaged, and upon
her

her replying in the affirmative, he rose to conduct his fair partner to the next chamber.

" I fear, Mr. Mackenzie," said Olivia, with genuine simplicity, " that you are not much flattered by mamma's comparing you to uncle Richard. Yet, I assure you, that he must have been extremely handsome when a young man, as I will convince you some day or other, by shewing you a miniature which he gave to mamma on his leaving England. I certainly think that you resemble the picture, which my poor uncle had painted for a lady to whom he was madly attached, and who abandoned him for another, although she had promised solemnly to be his."

" She must have been indeed unworthy such a love as that of your uncle," replied Edward gravely, " since the constancy of his passion appears still to affect his peace, and undermine his health. Mr. Colvill, though seen by me only for a few minutes, and evidently labouring under

G 3                indisposition,

indisposition, seems to be one of those characters who make an indelible impression on the mind. His form is dignified, his countenance, though saddened by the disappointments of his early years, is still calculated to charm; and his voice and manner have something in them *to me* peculiarly attractive. I should have thought that the woman who had once listened to the avowal of his tenderness, would never have heard with complacency the vows of another."

" I should have thought the same," said the lively Olivia, with unusual seriousness; " but my dear uncle was fated to love to distraction, and to love in vain. I never heard the name of the lady who so basely deceived him, but I believe that she is still living. I once thought that I had discovered it; but it might only be one of my own fancies."

Edward felt that he would give a great deal to be privy to this fancy of Olivia; yet of what moment to him could it possibly

sibly be, to be made acquainted with the name of the lady who had so cruelly blighted the happiness of Mr. Colvill's life?

Olivia now spoke of the Manninghams, and the heart of Edward beat quicker at the dear-loved sound. She had been one of the bridemaids to Constantia, and she now recapitulated to him, with good-natured willingness, the whole of the bridal ceremony. In doing this, she necessarily spoke of Flora, and this was a theme on which the charmed ear of Edward could have dwelt for ever. The tenderness of his feelings beamed in his glowing face, and his eyes, at once brilliant and languishing, were intently fixed on the countenance of Olivia, when a passing sigh removed them to the pale features of Flora, who at that instant moved forward with lord George ———.

A transient blush tinged the cheek of Flora, as she returned the embarrassed bow of Edward, and the familiar nod of his companion.

" That

" That is a dear sweet girl," exclaimed
Olivia, warmly, " and infinitely too good
for lord George : but I believe that things
are now nearly settled, and that my lovely friend will soon become the daughter
of a duke."

" Impossible !" cried Edward, hastily.

" And why impossible, Mr. Mackenzie?" inquired Olivia Osborne.

" I know not," said Edward, confusedly ;
" and yet I should have supposed that
neither sir Charles nor lady Manningham
would bestow their daughter upon one
whose only possible recommendation is
the greatness of his family connexions."

" Bless you !" exclaimed Olivia, laughingly ; " why, do you not know, Mr. Mackenzie, that now-a-days rank and fortune are
the two best recommendations that a young
man can produce in his favour ? What
parent, except indeed they possessed such
old-fashioned notions as mamma, would
decline the proposals of a duke's son ? No,
no, Mr. Mackenzie, such an offer is sure
of

of being received, though he that made it were little better than a knave or fool. I do not mean to insinuate that this is lord George's case; considering every thing, he is a decent kind of being, and I believe tolerably good-natured and obliging."

The eyes of Edward followed the sweet form of Flora until it was no longer visible.

The sigh which burst from his bosom was heard by Olivia.—" You pity Miss Manningham, Mr. Mackenzie; so do I: yet why should we consider her as an object of commiseration, when her own heart perhaps beats favourably for his lordship ?"

Edward started; then recovering himself, he said, in a faltering voice—" I have too high an opinion of sir Charles and lady Manningham to believe that they would force the inclinations of their daughter; if lord George is the received lover of Miss Manningham, it must be with her own consent."

They

They were now joined by Miss Osborne and her partner; and as they proceeded to the refreshment-room, Edward for a moment resigned the hand of Olivia, to speak to Frederic, whom he now for the first time perceived standing near his mother, who was seemingly in most earnest conversation with lady James Osborne and Mr. Colvill.

Could any thing at that moment have diffused the spirit of joyful hope into the soul of Edward, it would have been the kind and flattering attentions which he now met with from lady Manningham and her companions; but the bare supposition of Flora's being engaged to lord George —— had damped the buoyant and happy feelings of Mackenzie, who heard, with the languid smile of a disordered mind, that lady Jane ——, sister to lord George, had been inquiring after him repeatedly since she had met him at the house of sir Charles.

" You must dance with her ladyship to-night,

to-night, Edward," said lady Manningham, smilingly, " for I have ventured to promise for you. Lady Jane is an only daughter, and a spoiled one: she has taken a vast fancy to you; and therefore, trusting to your well-known gallantry, I assured her that you would feel yourself highly honoured by the possession of her fair hand. See, her ladyship advances towards us: ' I must spare her blushes.—Lady Jane, Mr. Mackenzie has been soliciting that my interest may be exerted to procure him the enviable distinction of becoming your partner for the ensuing dance, if you are not otherwise engaged.'"

The eyes of lady Jane sparkled with delight at this desirable piece of information, and she immediately assured Edward that she was at liberty to comply with his wishes, giving him at the same time a look of tender encouragement, which was perfectly sufficient to authorize a less diffident young man than Ed-

ward

ward to make the most of the present opportunity.

"I must just say a few words to my
dear Flora," said lady Jane, "and then, Mr.
Mackenzie, I will attend to you."

"Your ladyship does me infinite honour," replied Edward; "but may I be
permitted to accompany you?"

"Oh, most willingly," said lady Jane,
extending towards him her hand familiarly.

"I think that Edward's fortune is, already made," exclaimed lady Manningham, "if he does not mar it by his too-
scrupulous delicacy. Lady Jane is evidently charmed by his character and by
his appearance; she is perfectly her own
mistress, and may bestow her hand upon
whom she pleases."

"The chances are certainly in Edward's
favour," said Frederic, "but I doubt if he
will avail himself of her ladyship's partiality. He is too disinterested and too
generous a fellow to sacrifice his heart at
the shrine of WEALTH."

Lady

Lady James and her brother were now left alone for a few moments.—"I do not entirely approve of the present system of throwing young people in the way of each other," said she, gravely, " although it is acted upon by very worthy characters. For instance—lady Manningham has evidently introduced Mr. Mackenzie to lady Jane this evening, with the good-natured intention of giving him an opportunity to make the most of her ladyship's sentiments in his favour. I cannot bring myself to believe that a young man of such superior intellectual endowments will be induced to barter his future peace for the sake of rank and fortune."

"You speak, Maria, as if you had known Mr. Mackenzie for years," replied Mr. Colvill, thoughtfully : " how can you judge of his inclinations or his wishes upon so short an acquaintance ?"

" By his appearance, by the fire and brilliancy of his eyes, by the soul which beams in his countenance, my beloved brother,

ther, which is too like your own to en-
shrine a sordid or a selfish mind."

"Appearances are too often deceitful,
Maria; and this young man, all-interest-
ing, all candid as he seems, may be as
prone to evil as the matchless beauty
whose vicious inclinations ruined my hopes
and blighted my happiness, when I deemed it most secure from interruption."

"Ah, Richard! still harping on the
past, still anticipating future disappointments; and judging of human nature by
one who was a disgrace to her sex. I
thought, nay, indeed I expected, that you
would feel as highly interested for Mr.
Mackenzie as myself, and I am therefore
weak enough to be pained on finding that
my expectations are likely to prove vain."

"The interest which the sight of him
has occasioned *me* to feel," replied Mr.
Colvill, "I would fain have concealed within my own breast, lest I should a second
time have cause to lament my rashness
in trusting to appearances. Maria, rest satisfied

tisfied that I feel for your favourite all the kind sentiments with which your own friendly bosom abounds. There is a charm about his person, which cannot have influenced *your* feelings towards him, but which operated upon mine the moment I beheld him ; a charm———"

At that instant lady James felt herself called on to rise, in order to receive some fresh visitors, and Mr. Colvill quitted his seat and passed into the ball-room.

The pointed attentions of lady Jane, who was what might be called a fine young woman, joined to the freedom of her dress, which exposed to his eye the beauties of her person, soon had their due effect upon the senses of Edward. His spirits became buoyant, his conversation highly eloquent, and his countenance, of course, animated and fascinating.

Lady Jane viewed her companion with romantic admiration, and as she gazed on his handsome features, as she listened to his tuneful voice, she forgot the vast disparity

parity of their birth, and the probable cen-
sure of her relations, and seriously resolved to raise him to her own rank in life,
provided that no prior engagement on his
part existed to disappoint her wishes.

Flora beheld at a distance the conduct
of her brother's friend—beheld it with the
most saddened emotions of sorrow and regret. Not long before she had seen him
with Olivia Osborne, had seen him bestow on her those smiles of approving
kindness, which now he lavished on his
more exalted partner. Was Edward a
general lover, or was he attracted by the
splendour of lady Jane's family connexions, the glitter of her numerous jewels,
or by her own evident and marked partiality for himself?—" It must be the latter," thought Flora, sighing unconsciously
at the idea, " for Edward is too noble to be
biassed by any other feelings than those
of affection and gratitude."

Again that heavenly smile irradiated
the glowing countenance of Edward, and
Flora,

Flora, trembling and pale, gladly availed herself of lord George's proposal to take some refreshment.

" Upon my word," said his lordship, " Jane seems wonderfully pleased with her partner. Mackenzie is a fine young fellow, and I dare say infinitely diverting."

" He is very amiable," replied Flora, in a low voice, " and possesses talents which cannot fail to render his conversation pleasing."

Lady Jane and Edward now approached to where they were sitting. The former beckoned to her brother, who rising, politely offered his seat to Edward, while he attended the summons of his sister.

" George," said her ladyship, taking his arm, and leading him into the next apartment; " George, you must invite Mackenzie to call on you."

" Very well, Jane, I have no objection : but what do you mean to. do with him when he comes, for it will not be. in my power to entertain him ? Flora says that
he

he is so devilish clever, he will be too much for me."

"You silly fellow!" exclaimed lady Jane, "were it not for your good-nature, you would be intolerable. But do you invite Mr. Mackenzie to call on you as soon as possible, and I'll engage to amuse him."

"Silly as you think me, Jane," retorted his lordship, "I am wise enough to perceive the drift of your meaning. Mackenzie is a handsome young fellow, and you are your own mistress. You understand me, Jane?"

While his sensible lordship was talking to her cunning ladyship, Edward, placed by the side of Flora Manningham, was endeavouring to draw her into conversation; but he found her unusually reserved, and, as he imagined, cold and distant. His pride took the alarm, and rising hastily from his seat, as he perceived lady Jane and her brother re-enter the refreshment-room, he joined them with an apparent eagerness,

eagerness, which more than confirmed the suspicions of Flora, that lady Jane had succeeded in attaching him to her list of danglers.

Lord George, according to his instructions, was so extremely earnest in pressing Edward to call on him the next day, that the latter found it impossible to refuse, and thus lady Jane obtained her object, which was to gain a favourable opportunity of introducing Edward to her father, the duke of ———.

Lady Jane was satisfied with her night's amusement, and as the morning was now far advanced, she signified her wish to retire.

Edward led her to her carriage, and if he ventured too warmly to press her unreluctant hand in his (let it be remembered that he was not yet nineteen, and that the attractions of lady Jane were such as might have thawed a colder bosom than that of Mackenzie), the eyes of lady Jane told him that his boldness was forgiven—

nay

nay more, that it was not displeasing to
her; and Edward's gratitude was thus
awakened by the flattering notice which
he had received from one so high and nobly
born as her ladyship.

## CHAPTER VII.

EDWARD had not left his bedchamber the
next day, when Frederic Manningham
paid him a visit.—" I am come, my dear
Mackenzie," said he, " to have half an
hour's conversation with you, upon a subject which materially affects my peace.
Your opinion may be of use to me; at all
events, as the happiness of Flora is con-
cerned, it is natural that I should impart
my uneasiness to you, who feel nearly as
much interested as myself in her welfare."

" What can have disturbed the repose
of Miss Manningham," inquired Edward
gravely,

gravely, "when she can boast the possession of such a lover as lord George ——?"

"*Such* a lover!" exclaimed Frederic
scornfully. "I will not, cannot believe
that Flora is attached to a butterfly like
his lordship. But what makes me uneasy,
Mackenzie, is the alteration which has
lately taken place in the spirits and manners of my sister. You know what a little lively creature she was before she was
introduced, how frequently she smiled, and
what delight her smiles imparted to us all.
Now she is silent and thoughtful, even to
melancholy, and seldom smiles, or if she
does, her smiles are evidently forced—they
come not as usual from her light and happy heart; and my only fear is, that some
secret grief preys upon her mind, and un-
dermines her peace. I know that my father and mother are favourable to the attentions of lord George; but I know also,
that they would not force the inclinations
of my sister, were she averse to the union.
What,

What, therefore, dear Mackenzie, can oppress the heart of our beloved Flora?"

"I know not," replied Edward, with a sigh, "what hidden sorrow can affect the peace of Miss Manningham, but none can deplore more sincerely than myself, that any cause should exist to occasion her a moment's uneasiness."

"I believe you, my friend, and therefore have taken this early opportunity to impart to you my fears on her account. The mind of Flora is of so superior a kind, that it is next to impossible that she should feel any thing like an affection for so weak and insipid a character as lord George. He is good-natured and friendly in the extreme, but that is all—his intellects are below mediocrity; and when I see him the constant companion of my sister, I almost feel inclined to quarrel with him for his constancy, and to reproach Flora for her tacit encouragement of his addresses."

"And why, my dear Frederic, should you

you do either," said Edward, " since lord
George cannot be as insignificant in the
eyes of your sister as he is in yours? I
did not perceive any uneasiness or discontent in Miss Manningham last night. His
lordship, as usual, was her devoted admirer,
and she seemed perfectly satisfied and
pleased that he was so. I rather think that
your imagination, my friend, has been on
this occasion too busy in conjuring up a
subject to torment you, and that Miss Manningham is as cheerful and as contented as
formerly."

" Oh no, I am not apt to imagine sorrows—not apt to conjure up sources of uneasiness to myself; as yet the world has
too many charms, which sweeten my existence; and I at first refused to admit the
idea of Flora's being unhappy, until I had
repeatedly found her in tears, and as repeatedly heard her decline confiding to me
the cause. Flora would not weep for fancied griefs, nor conceal her secret unhappiness from me, without some serious reason.

son. Mackenzie, you are more eloquent, more persuasive than I am; you also possess great influence over Flora: if *you* urge her to confide to you the cause of those tears which she has vainly endeavoured to hide from her brother, she may be more communicative to you than she has been to me."

"Heavens!" exclaimed Edward, in agitation, "what a request have you made! How can I, with any degree of propriety, hint to Miss Manningham my knowledge of so delicate a circumstance as that of her being unhappy?—What right have I to pry into a sorrow which, if real, ought to be sacred from the eye of curiosity. No, Frederic, I dare not venture to address Miss Manningham upon a subject which she seeks to conceal from the tenderest and best of brothers."

"I did not expect, Mackenzie, that you would refuse my request," said Frederic; half angry at the disappointment of his wishes; "but you have ceased to feel that
brotherly

brotherly interest in what concerns my sister, since you have mingled with the world."

"You wrong me, Frederic," replied Edward, with some degree of warmth; "it is not *I* who have changed, it is your *sister*. No more, as formerly; does she greet my approach with a friendly smile, or extend her hand to welcome my arrival. Miss Manningham both looks and speaks with the chilling tone of indifference; or if she smiles or extends her hand, it is to meet the tender pressure of lord George, whose constant attendance even excludes the usual attentions of her older acquaintance."

"I see that I am not likely to receive any assistance from you, Mackenzie," said Frederic, rising to take leave, "therefore I will not detain you from your breakfast."

"Will you stay and partake of it with me?" asked Edward, in a conciliating tone. "Mr. Lindsay will be happy to see you;

or, if you like, I will order Oliver to bring our coffee into my painting-room."

" I should be glad to see Mr. Lindsay," replied Frederic, " but I fear the sight of me would give rise to painful reflections, connected with his daughter.; therefore I must decline your invitation. Charles has written to his father, beseeching him to forgive his conduct, and to attribute it to any thing but a disregard of his anger. My father read us the letter and his own answer. The last was short and sufficiently cutting. He alluded most strongly to the unfeeling indelicacy of Clara in quitting her dying mother; ' but,' said he, ' as I feel convinced that her fault, like your own, will bring with it its own punishment, I will not add to the keenness of your feelings by closing my doors against your approach. They shall be open to receive you, Charles; but the reception which your wife may experience from my family will entirely depend on her own good conduct.

duct... May the virtues of the wife atone, if possible, for the failings of the daughter!' Such were the words of my father; how they will be relished by my mad-brained brother and his heartless wife, I know not; but of this I am assured, that if she has the impudence to accompany Charles in his visit to our house, she will not wish to enter it a second time, for my mother is resolved to express in the strongest terms her disapprobation of the past."

"If so," said Edward, " it is not very probable that she will attempt a reconciliation, a second time, unless her husband may possess more power over her than any other being ever did. Poor Mr. Lindsay continues deeply affected by her cruel desertion, and, unless some change takes place to remove him to a different scene, I fear that he will not long survive his wife. He remains inexorable, as to seeing or receiving any communication from his daughter, and all the hope I now have is, that his uncle in Ireland may invite him to pass the

summer

summer at his estate, where the convivial
disposition and known hospitality of the
Irish families may contribute to divert his
mind from the painful subject of Clara's
unnatural elopement. I have wished, for
this fortnight past, to take a hasty journey
down to Monmouthshire, but my reluctance to leaving him alone has prevented
me."

"And what, Mackenzie, can possibly
call you into Monmouthshire?" inquired
Frederic. "I never heard you mention
that you had friends in that county."

"Have you then forgotten," said Edward, "what I told you respecting the so-
lemn request of the young son of the marchioness of Anendale, which was that I
should, in case of his death, convey to his
sister, lady Elinor, a lock of his hair, which
he gave to me for that purpose? I should
have fulfilled my promise before now, but
for the reason I have just stated."

"Lady Elinor is my second cousin, I
believe," said Frederic. "I have heard
much

much of the beauty and grace of her mother, and I feel some curiosity to learn whether her daughter is equally attractive;
but I am not likely to have it gratified, as
I find that, although she is nearly seventeen, she is not to be introduced until the
winter after next. There is a degree of
cruelty in thus keeping lady Elinor secluded in an old Gothic mansion, with no
other society than her governess, which
gives me a very unfavourable opinion of
the maternal affection of lady Anendale;
and I should enjoy nothing more, my dear
Edward, than accompanying you in your
journey, that I might have an opportunity
of seeing this poor neglected girl, with
whom my heart claimed kindred the moment you told me of her situation, as it
was described to you by her affectionate
little brother."

'"Edward was overjoyed at the proposal
of Frederic, and promised, if possible, to
take the journey in the course of the ensuing week, could he but be certain that

Mr.

Mr. Lindsay would not materially feel the loss of his society.

"If we travel post," said Frederic, "we can be there and back again in less than three days. I never felt so great an eagerness to behold any human being as I now do to see lady Elinor. Poor girl! what a shame to immure her within the walls of an old gloomy castle, and at an age when other young women are privileged to enjoy all the gaieties of life. It would be capital sport to cheat the vigilance of her mother, and run away with the girl whom she is pleased to consider as yet too young to mix with the world. I rather suspect that the marchioness is apprehensive lest the beauty of the daughter should eclipse the fading charms of the mother."

"Stay till you have seen the marchioness of Anendale," said Edward, with a sigh which he could not repress; "and then, Frederic, you will blush at having called those beauties faded which are even now at the height of their attractive loveliness.

liness. Lady Elinor may be handsome, but she can never equal, much less eclipse her mother."

Frederic looked intently in the face of Edward, which immediately became of a deeper crimson.—"We shall see, my friend," he exclaimed, " and I trust see shortly, the pretensions of lady Elinor to rival her mother. I must contrive to catch a glimpse of the marchioness when she returns to England."

" Then you will think as I do," replied Edward.

".I am not quite sure that I shall think as *warmly* as you do, Mackenzie," said Frederic, archly ; " but, at all events, hurry your journey as much as possible, for I am dying to assure lady Elinor of my kind wishes for her emancipation from her prison-house."

He now took leave of Edward, who descended to the apartment of Mr. Lindsay.

The father of Clara had been up several hours, but he would not suffer Edward to

be

be disturbed; as he concluded it was morning before he returned from lady James
Osborne's. He therefore breakfasted alone,
Mary Mackenzie being engaged with her
mother in arranging the different fruits,
placing flowers between them, that they
might appear to the best advantage.

When Edward entered their little drawing-
ing-room, Mr. Lindsay inquired if he had
been amused with his evening's entertain-
ment, and listened with much seeming
attention to Edward's lively description
of what had passed; yet, at the mention
of the name of Manningham, a sigh escaped him, as it brought to his recollection the child who had so cruelly deserted
him, when he stood most in need of her
consolation and support.

During this conversation, Edward contrived to introduce the subject of his promise to the young earl, and his own wish
that he might be enabled to perform it before the return of the marchioness to England.

Mr.

Mr. Lindsay, who always considered a promise to be sacred, instantly advised him to take the earliest opportunity of visiting Monmouthshire, lest any unforeseen accident might delay or prevent his seeing lady Elinor.

Edward thus advised, agreed to leave town in the course of a week, during which time he should finish a picture which he had nearly executed for a friend of sir Joseph Rennie's, from the profits of which he intended to remit to Mr. Curwen the ten pounds he had advanced him.

Remembering his engagement to call on lord George ——, Edward, who knew that the best part of the day would be gone before he could return home, resolved to pay several necessary visits, in order that his hours of study might not be broken into the ensuing week. He therefore proceeded to the mansion of the duke of ——, in St. James's-square, where he was evidently expected by the porter, who seemed acquainted with his name. 'Four

servants,

servants, in dashing liveries, were standing idle in the hall, one of whom ushered Edward into a magnificent apartment, where lord George and his sister welcomed his arrival, the former with an extended hand, and the latter with the sweetest smiles which she could command.

Lord George asked a few questions relative to the weather, and other commonplace topics of conversation, and then left his sister to *entertain* his visitor, while he *entertained* himself with a couple of large spaniel dogs, who lay on each side of him, on a beautiful couch, richly carved, and supported by gilt figures.

Lady Jane, however, seemed not to be in want of her brother's assistance. She had a tolerable knowledge of all the new publications, at least of poetry, plays, and novels, which constitute the chief of a lady's library. Then she endeavoured to find out the kind of music most liked by Edward, who was a passionate admirer of the harp, upon which she played with

superior

superior skill; and upon learning which was his favourite instrument, lady Jane, purposely inquired if he had heard a new song, naming one, which Edward requested her to favour him with.

Lady Jane cheerfully complied, and placing herself so as to shew the graceful *contour* of her form, she sang, in a fine melodious voice, the following words, while her eyes betrayed to the attentive Edward, that her heart was no stranger to the passion which her tongue described:

### SONG.

" 'Tis hard, when summer clothes the year
 In nature's gayest dress,
The vigorous morn of life to wear
 In study's dull recess

'Tis hard, with an indignant breast,
 Betray'd by secret wiles,
To meet the spoiler of its rest,
 And deck the brow in smiles.

But, oh! 'tis harder to conceal
 A lover's pregnant sigh;
And what the secret heart doth feel,
 To bid the cheek deny."

H 6                    Edward

Edward was charmed, and lady Jane was perfectly satisfied with the demonstrations of his approbation. She invited him to accompany her to the opera, saying, that she was engaged to call for the Manninghams that evening, and if he liked, her carriage should 'stop' and take him up.

Edward coloured as he remembered that his lodgings were not in a part of the town sufficiently fashionable to admit of a duke's carriage stopping at his door ; he therefore declined this last mark of her condescension, promising to join her at the opera-house.

They were now interrupted by the entrance of the duke, to whom lady Jane immediately introduced Edward, as a particular friend of her brother George.

His grace received him with courtly politeness, and upon learning his talent for painting, good-naturedly offered to shew him the few pictures which his town-house contained, an offer highly gratify-

ing

ing to Edward, who thus obtained a sight of some of the finest productions of foreign art.

On taking leave, lady Jane reminded him of his engagement for the evening; and lord George now thought proper to second the wishes of his sister, by saying that he hoped Edward would not forget to join them; for that he knew that his presence would be a most agreeable surprise to his very dear friend Frederic Manningham.

" So, if you see Frederic," said lord George, "" don't tell him that you are to have a seat in our box, or don't say that you will be there at all. That will be the best, won't it, Jane ?"

"" If you wish to *surprise* Mr. Manningham, it certainly will," replied her ladyship, smiling expressively on Edward, who now took leave, and proceeded to make the different calls which he had intended. Sir Joseph Rennie was not forgotten. He

was

was at home, and sincerely glad to see that his young friend had returned to town.

Almost his first inquiry was, if he had changed his opinion of the marchioness of Anendale? to which Edward replied, that he feared she was not quite as faultless as he had hoped.

. Sir Joseph then asked for his address, and upon receiving it, remarked that Edward must remove to a more fashionable part of the town, as it was necessary that his residence should be such as would allow of his receiving visitors of rank, who might wish to converse with him upon the subject of any picture they might choose him to execute.

Edward saw in an instant the propriety of sir Joseph's observation, and, much as he regretted being obliged to leave the friendly Mrs. Alexander Mackenzie, yet he acknowledged that his future prospects required that in this case he should sacrifice inclination to interest. He therefore promised

promised sir Joseph to remove almost immediately, while the former appointed him to dine with him the next day, that he might meet a gentleman who had expressed a desire to see him, in order, that he might explain to him the subject of a picture which he wished to have painted for his own private chapel.

The heart of Edward now glowed with the warmest sensations of pleasure, at the prospect of a work which would add so considerably to his finances, as well as increase his growing fame. By this he should be enabled to retain in his service the worthy Oliver, and to procure additional comforts for Mr. Lindsay.

Shortening the rest of his visits, he hurried back to impart the pleasing intelligence of his unexpected good fortune, which gave the purest satisfaction to his melancholy friend, and which nearly drove poor Oliver out of his senses. So great was his joy, upon learning that he was not to be dismissed by Edward, that he actually

wept

wept like a child, and it was several hours
before he could talk rationally to the master whom he so dearly loved, and who
could not help being sensibly affected himself at the proofs of an attachment at once
disinterested and tender.

## CHAPTER IX.

EDWARD was in high spirits, and his animated features expressed the delighted
state of his feelings when he entered the
box of the duke of ———, at the opera-
house. The Manninghams, with lord
George and his sister, were already there:
a glance from the eyes of the latter directed
Edward to take his station behind the
chair of lady Jane, who, nodding to him
familiarly, said, in a loud whisper, that she
was half inclined to quarrel with him for
being so late.

Edward

Edward bent over to make his peace with her ladyship, and a smile quickly proclaimed that her anger was of short duration.

Lord George pleased himself with witnessing the agreeable surprise of Frederic, on the appearance of his friend.—" Ah, I knew that you would be glad to see him," said his lordship; " so I told him not to say a word about his being engaged to meet Jane at the opera to-night."

" I am always happy to see Mackenzie in all places, and at all times," replied Frederic; " therefore, my lord, I can say with sincerity, that you have obliged *me* by inviting him to meet us here."

" Oh, don't thank me," exclaimed his lordship, loud enough for Flora to hear; " it was not I, but Jane, who invited Mr. Mackenzie—not but that I like him very much, only I did not think of telling him, as she did, that he was welcome to a seat in our box as often as he pleased. Jane is wonderfully taken with him; and upon

my

my soul, I must say that he is a fine fellow, and deserves to be made a duke.";

"He is in a fair way to raise himself,"
whispered Frederic, leaning over Flora
as he spoke. "I think that lady Jane
has both sense and discernment to reward
the talents of my friend : but what will
the duke say to his daughter's choice?"

"Jane is her own mistress," replied lord
George, "and will not consult any one
upon that subject. My father knows her
temper, and never opposes her; and for
my part, she is so completely my master,
that I never venture to contradict her in
any thing."

Flora, pale as the first timid flower of
spring, scarce breathed during this important dialogue between her brother and her
acknowledged lover. Her heart throbbed
with convulsive motion, as she turned her
modest eyes towards Edward and his noble
enslaver. A smile of seeming happiness
played round his mouth, and rendered his
features doubly handsome. His graceful
body,

body, half bent to catch the flattering praise which lady Jane was repeating to him, word for word as it came from the lips of lady James Osborne, who had call-ed that morning soon after his departure, and to whom she was engaged that night to return home to supper.

The box of lady James was nearly oppo-site to that of the duke. Her ladyship was absent, but her daughters and Mr. Colvill were there; and Flora had observ-ed, with some degree of surprise, that the attention of their uncle, instead of being directed to the performance, was wholly taken up by watching the movements of Edward and lady Jane.

Flora sighed, as she felt convinced that Mr. Colvill's ideas were similar to her own.—" He has observed, and therefore knows more of the world than I do," thought Flora, " and it is evident that he considers them as attached to each other. Why should I wish to mar the brilliant prospects of my dear brother's friend—I,

whom

whom my parents have destined for another?"

Flora turned her mild eyes towards lord George; a tear rushed into each—a blush of conscious secret shame, the shame of jarring feelings, of contending duties, tinged the fair cheek of Flora. A look from her mother heightened the glow.—" I yield to my fate," thought Flora; " and if it wills me to be miserable, I shall at least have the consolation of knowing that I have obeyed the wishes of those who gave me being—that I have fulfilled *their* hopes, though I shall annihilate my own."

Edward, though the chief of his attention was engrossed by lady Jane, found leisure to impart to Frederic the joyful intelligence, that he should be at liberty to gratify his desires early the next week; a piece of news which gave great satisfaction to his impatient friend, who actually felt restless and uneasy to behold his fair relation.

Edward had likewise encountered frequently the gaze of Mr. Colvill; and he could

could not avoid feeling some degree of curiosity to learn the reason why he so evidently watched all his movements, when his attention ought naturally to be directed towards the representation, which was one of the most celebrated of the Italian operas. In any other person this conduct he would have deemed impertinent, but Edward felt a respect, as well as an earnest desire to gain the esteem of lady Osborne's melancholy brother, which prevented his being offended by a scrutiny that appeared more singular than offensive.

Edward also twice attempted to draw Flora Manningham into conversation, but she seemed so painfully reserved, so strangely shy of replying to his questions, that he gave up all hope of hearing fall from her lips that night any other words than a few monosyllables, uttered in so low and faltering a tone, that Edward's quick and attentive ear could scarcely catch the sounds as they murmuring passed.—"Ah," thought Edward, "she no longer feels that tender friendship

friendship which every look and word used formerly to evince. Flora of the Hall, and Flora of London, are two distinct beings. The splendour of a coronet, the prospect of a ducal alliance, has more charms for Flora now than the pleasing recollections of our early years. I am I too humbly born, too poorly fortuned, to be an object of consideration in the dazzled eyes of Flora. Yet, humble as are my connexions, poor as are my fortunes, the high-souled daughter of a duke does not disdain to court my smiles, to seek my friendship, and to honour me with her good opinion."

Edward withdrew his eyes from the bashful blushing Flora, and turning them quickly on lady Jane, who at that instant touched his arm with her fan, he felt all the warm gratitude of his nature called into action, as he contrasted the different manners of his noble admirer with those of the altered and repulsive Flora. Edward, with a glowing countenance, and eyes plainly expressive of his feelings, pressed

ed the soft unreluctant hand of lady Jane
within his own.

" You will accompany me and George
to lady James's supper-party ?" said she,
in a voice of tenderness which soothed the
mortified pride of Edward. " I know,
Mackenzie, that *you* will, always be a welcome guest at *her* table." 

" I can refuse your ladyship nothing,"
said Edward expressively, " and shall
think myself too happy in being allowed
to accompany you."

At that moment Edward caught the inquiring eye of Mr. Colvill, fixed intently on
himself. He knew not why, but he felt his
colour deepen, and an awkward sensation
pervaded his frame. Lady Jane addressed
him, and again he listened, again he smiled;
but still the effect remained of Mr. Colvill's inquiring glance.

At the conclusion of the opera, the Miss
Osbornes and their uncle came round to
the duke's box, and endeavoured to persuade lady Manningham to return and sup
with

with their mother; but this her ladyship declined, pleading herself already engaged to look in at another fashionable rout in Bruton-street.

" And are you also engaged, Mr. Mackenzie?" said Miss Osborne.

Before Edward could reply, lady Jane said—" I can answer, Maria, for Mr. Mackenzie, since, relying upon your mother's esteem for him, I have engaged him to accompany me to Osborne House, where I am confident he will be received as a welcome visitor."

" Your ladyship seems to have formed a proper estimate of our kind feelings towards Mr. Mackenzie," replied Mr. Colvill. Then turning to Edward, and offering him his hand—" I feel," said he, " greatly indebted to lady Jane for the opportunity she has thus given me of seeing you again.

that I may call on you."

The servants now came to announce that the carriages were waiting. Lord George

George conducted Flora to that of her father, while Frederic, presenting his arm
to lady Manningham, whispered to Edward that he would see him to-morrow.

His friend had only time to reply that
he should be at home the whole of the day,
when lady Jane motioned to leave the
box, and Edward felt himself called upon
to hand her to her carriage, though Mr.
Colvill was evidently on the point of offering his assistance. He smiled good-naturedly, though faintly, as her ladyship took
the arm of Edward, saying, as she passed
—" I must not complain, lady Jane, at
your preferring a younger arm than mine;
Mr. Mackenzie has a prior claim to the
honour of your attention."

" Another time, Mr. Colvill," replied
lady Jane, " and I shall feel myself highly
honoured by engrossing yours."

They were now met on the stairs by
lord George, with whom they immediately proceeded to the duke's carriage, while

Mr. Colvill led his nieces to that of lady James.

In a few minutes the party stopped at Osborne House, where the flattering kindness of its amiable owner soon convinced Edward that he was indeed a welcome visitor.

Her ladyship now introduced him for the first time to her husband, who had arrived that morning from Ireland, and who appeared equally disposed as her ladyship to pay the homage which is ever due to exalted merit and superior talent.

Edward was charmed with the affability and good-humoured pleasantry of his lordship, who, on his part, had not his duty to his guests prevented him, would have conversed the chief of the evening with our young artist, while the sweetly benevolent countenance of lady James expressed her delight at seeing the perfect coincidence which there appeared to be between her lord's feelings and her own.

" How is it, dearest Richard," said her ladyship, " that Osborne has entered more warmly

warmly into my sentiments than you? See with what willingness he gives credit to my character of young Mackenzie: it was but this instant that he told me that he thought his resemblance to you became more strikihg the more he conversed with him, and that he was determined to exert all his interest to bring him forward in his profession. I have not heard half as much from you, my dear brother, and yet it is not your general conduct to act so tamely, when *I* feel so warmly."

"I am not what I *was*," said Mr. Colvill, pensively. "For once, beloved Maria, you are deceived in the sentiments which your young friend has excited; they are such as I dare not give way to, lest I should be again deceived—again made wretched. But tell me what you wish me to do for him, Maria: shall I adopt him as my own?"

"If your heart can love him as you would do your own son, if you had one, I say yes, my brother. I will be the pledge

for Mackenzie's being worthy of such an
election.  He will no more deceive me
than you have done, my Richard."

Mr. Colvill gave a sudden start;  then as
suddenly recovering himself, he said—
" Generous, noble Maria, thus to plead
against the interests of your own children,
in favour of one whose chief merit, in *your*
eyes, is his imaginary resemblance to your
brother!  Imaginary it must indeed be,
my love, for who but yourself or the worthy Osborne could compare the fire and
brilliancy of Mackenzie's eyes with the
faded melancholy hue of mine?   The fine
regularity of his features, but above all,
his smile—his to *me* magic smile, destroys
at once the fancied likeness."

" Ah, Richard!" exclaimed lady James,
in a voice of tender recollection—" ah,
Richard, it is not what you *are*, but what
you *were* at his age, that forms the resemblance between Mackenzie and yourself.  Affliction may have damped the
once-dazzling brilliancy of your eyes, but
the

the colour and the expression of the heart's tenderest feelings are the same. The warm sunny glow of health and joy tinge the features of my favourite, while yours are pale, my brother, not from age, but from sorrow concealed. Yet the form of his face, and the general resemblance, has struck more than Osborne and myself. His pliant figure, his easy graceful movements, his laugh, his voice—all, all are like what you, my Richard, were when you left England nineteen years ago."

Mr. Colvill mused for a moment, then hastily exclaimed—" And wherefore this resemblance, Maria? What do you infer from it?"—A smile of bitterness, of suppressed agony, passed over his features—" There are enough, my sister, to vouch that Mackenzie is no relation to my family."

Edward at that instant came up to them.—" I fear that I intrude," said he, respectfully bowing to lady James ; " but Miss Osborne requested me to inform your

ladyship

ladyship that your presence is wanting in the second card-room."

" *You* can never be considered in the light of an intruder," replied lady James, rising and offering him her place, which he immediately occupied. " In this instance you have the power of obliging me," continued her ladyship, " by endeavouring to divert the mind of my dear brother, who feels but little amusement in scenes like the present."

" I shall indeed feel proudly happy," said Edward, " if through me Mr. Colvill can receive any gratification, however slight it may be."

" You are too good, Mr. Mackenzie," replied the brother of lady James, at the same time pressing his hand, " thus voluntarily to devote to one who is half a misanthrope those moments which might be rendered precious if passed in the society of another: but I will not waste them in giving you cause to regret your good-nature, by reverting to the subject of my

own

own private misfortunes. My sister, who is one of the best of human beings, has imparted to me the lively interest which she feels for your welfare. My feelings are in unison with her own. It may be in my power to serve you, Mr. Mackenzie, in your professional capacity; but as this is neither a proper time nor place for serious communications, if you will allow me, I will call some morning at your lodgings: I should like to take a peep into your painting-room; or, if you prefer it, will you name a day when you can come and breakfast with me? At present I am with lady James Osborne."

Edward presented Mr. Colvill with a card of his address, saying at the same time, that he should remove in the course of a week or ten days to a more convenient part of the town; but that he should be happy to see Mr. Colvill any morning when it was convenient, or to wait upon him at Osborne House.

" Then I will call on you to-morrow,"

said

said Mr. Colvill, looking at the card as he spoke, " for I have not yet been so fortunate as to gain a sight of any of your productions." He now purposely changed the conversation to another subject, until he led to that which he conceived to be nearest to the heart of Edward. He spoke of lady Jane, and the nobleness of her connexions, and the greatness of her family's interest; but the cheek of Edward did not assume a deeper hue at the mention of her name, for he at that moment had forgotten the inquiring glances of the speaker directed to himself at the opera house; and thus, from the steadiness of his look and manner, Mr. Colvill was at a loss to decide how far his feelings were engaged in the cause of lady Jane.

They were now interrupted, and Mr. Colvill, from necessity, postponed until another opportunity the scrutiny he meant to make—a scrutiny which, in any other person, would have been grossly indelicate, but which in him, situated as he was, and under

under the influence of the most generous and noble sentiments, and guided by the purest motives of regard for Edward, and tenderness for his favourite sister lady James, could not be called indelicate or prying. It was necessary that he should ascertain the fact of Edward's disengaged affections before he could bring about the plan he meditated for his future good.

From the first time of Mr. Colvill's introduction to Edward, and his perfect knowledge of the partiality which lady James entertained for him, this plan had occupied the chief of his leisure reflections. He was in fact more warmly interested in the fate of Edward than he chose to acknowledge, lest, after the severe disappointment which he had met with at his first entrance into the world, he might be accused of rashness and inexperience, in thus hastily adopting the opinions and sentiments of a warm-hearted and romantic woman.

Mr. Colvill had no sooner beheld the ob-

ject

jeet of his sister's eulogiums, than his heart did justice to her praise, and, in spite of its early misfortunes, expanded towards Edward with a kindness equal to her own. With his usual quickness of decision, he instantly formed the plan of seconding the wishes of lady James, by promoting the fortunes of her favourite. He imagined that he perceived in his youngest niece, Olivia, a secret inclination towards Edward, which he was confident lady James would not disapprove; and it was therefore his intention, in case of a mutual inclination being discovered in Edward, to bestow on the young couple a considerable share of his large fortune, with this proviso, that Edward should take his name. By this means he would amply provide for the *eléve* of his sister without injuring her daughters, and perpetuate his name, which might otherwise become extinct, as his only surviving brother had no male heir to inherit his property.

Mr. Colvill, however, felt that his plan was

was uncertain, and that its accomplishment was rendered doubtful by the preference which lady Jane —— so evidently
betrayed for Edward. He had watched,
with an anxiety somewhat painful, the conduct of Edward towards her ladyship at
the opera house; yet still he remained
uncertain what construction to put upon
the looks and manners of our young artist,.
as both might be influenced by the pride
of gratified vanity, and by the consciousness
of knowing that he was an object of importance in the eyes of a handsome girl, so
nobly connected as lady Jane. Before,
therefore, Mr. Colvill imparted his plan
to lady James, he was desirous of learning
its practicability; and of gaining the necessary information, if possible, from Edward's self, whether it was gratitude or
love that attached him to lady Jane ——..

To obtain so delicate a piece of information, was now the chief consideration of
Mr. Colvill; yet his knowledge of Edward
was slight, and the confidence he wished

was

was only the reward of long-tried friend-ship. However, the attempt must be made; and with this view he inquired his address, resolving to gain his good opinion and esteem, as the first step towards merit-ing his confidence. Accordingly, the next day, Mr. Colvill called at the lodgings of Edward, and found him engaged in his painting-room, adding the last touches to a picture of considerable merit.

Struck with the beauty of the perform-ance, Mr. Colvill expressed his admiration in terms highly gratifying to the artist, who displayed a modesty so unusual, yet so pleasing, that it enhanced the value of his work, stamping it with double worth in the eyes of Mr. Colvill, who inquired when he should be at leisure to begin a series of pictures from sketches which he had him-self taken, and brought over with him, of Indian scenery.

"I intend," said Mr. Colvill, "as soon as I can find a house to suit my taste, to fill up one suite of apartments in the In-

dian

dian costume; you will therefore oblige
me by calling when you have time, and
then you can examine the drawings, which
I am anxious to have copied, if possible,
under my own direction, as the hints and
descriptions which I shall be enabled to
give you will greatly assist your compre-
hension of my own views. As I shall,
therefore, engross a large proportion of
your time, Mr. Mackenzie, and prevent
your undertaking any other work of consequence, you must allow *me* to set a value
upon both your time and occupation, as in
this instance I believe that I am a better
judge than yourself."

"I shall be perfectly satisfied, sir," said
Edward, " to leave what you mention entirely to yourself; while on my part I shall
be more than repaid, if I am so fortunate
as to answer your expectations."

He then informed him of his engagement to dine the next day with sir Joseph
Rennie, who was at the same to introduce
him to a gentleman, to whom sir Joseph
had

had partly promised that he should paint an altar-piece for his private chapel; "but," said Edward, " I will endeavour to decline the work if I can, that I may be wholly at liberty to devote all my attention to the subject of your sketches."

"I thank you," replied Mr. Colvill, "and shall consider myself as obliged by your undertaking them as soon as possible—not that I mean to fag you to death," added he, smilingly, " only that I shall feel at ease respecting them, as soon as I shall know that you have begun them; and as there are eight views, it may not be amiss, Mr. Mackenzie, if I just mention to you, that I have valued the time and trouble of their execution at two thousand guineas, a sum which may fall short of their merits, but which may act as a stimulus to so young a man as yourself, particularly as it may only be the forerunner of a nobler recompence, should your circumstances allow of the fulfilment of my hopes. Do not pain me, my dear Mr. Mackenzie, by any expression

expression of thanks. I am interested, warmly interested in your concerns. My sister's friendly sentiments you are already acquainted with; *they* alone would influence my feelings and actions, but you possess a stronger, a more irresistible claim to my regard than even *her* tender recommendation—a claim of which she is wholly ignorant. Dear as she is, and ever has been to my soul, yet there are some circumstances relative to my early disappointments, which I neither *could* nor *would* impart to her."

Mr. Colvill looked greatly agitated; he took the hand of Edward, who evidently sympathized in his feelings, although ignorant of the cause which occasioned his emotion.—" Mackenzie, we must be better acquainted," said Mr. Colvill, trying to recover his self-command. " You have the power—yes, I feel that *you* alone possess the power of sweetening the remainder of my existence, and of rendering life still worthy of preserving."

" Only

" Only tell me *how*," exclaimed Edward, as he warmly pressed the hand that grasped his own, " only tell me *how*, and I shall deem myself blest indeed, my dear sir, if through me you can receive one moment's happiness. Oh, do not doubt my sincerity! I am young—I am inexperienced, but I am capable of proving to what extent a grateful mind and an affectionate heart can go."

. " *I will not doubt you,* Mackenzie," said Mr. Colvill, in an agitated voice, although fate should doom me to a second disappointment, where my heart had placed its fondest hopes. No, Mackenzie, I will not doubt you; I will believe, that although you are young, perhaps ambitious, perhaps even thoughtless, as youth too frequently is, yet I will believe, Mackenzie, that you are sincere in your present feelings, and that you will be equally sincere in your affection—I will believe this, because you are not a woman."

Mr. Colvill leaned against the shoulder of

of Edward for support, who was scarcely less agitated than himself. At length he recovered his composure.—" Forgive me, my dear Mackenzie," said he, tenderly regarding his expressive countenance; " I have suffered myself to be surprised into a weakness of which I feel myself ashamed; but I trust to your honour to hold my sorrows sacred. When shall I see you?"

Edward replied that he would call at Osborne House after he quitted sir Joseph Rennie, if Mr. Colvill was disengaged.

" Do so, my young friend," said Mr. Colvill, " for I shall be at home, and alone."

He then took a hasty leave of Edward, who silently followed him to his carriage, which was waiting at the door of Mrs. Alexander Mackenzie.

CHAP-

# CHAPTER X.

THE visit of Mr. Colvill gave rise to a train
of new ideas in the mind of Edward. How
could he possibly account for the mysterious agitation he had betrayed, or for the
equally mysterious confession which had
escaped the lips of Mr. Colvill during
that agitation? What claim could the
son of Alice Mackenzie have upon the
good offices and friendly sentiments of the
brother of lady James Osborne? Edward
recollected that his mother had said that
he was like his father: perhaps that father,
whose name she so sacredly concealed, was
a dear-loved friend, or near relation of Mr.
Colvill; perhaps—but how fruitless were
his suppositions, how vain his conjectures,
unless indeed that he could obtain the
long-wished for knowledge of who was
his

his real father! That alone appeared wanting to unravel all the mystery of his birth, the agitation of Mr. Colvill, and the flattering kindness of lady James Osborne, as well as the sudden paleness of the beautiful marchioness upon his first introduction to her. But what could explain the nature and the cause of his own feelings—tender, enthusiastic, and conquering his better judgment, which vainly combatted against the force and power of lady Anendale's influence over his senses?

This was a subject on which Edward could form no decided opinion. The more he reflected on it, the more he grew bewildered, impatient, and unhappy; and, had not his ideas of filial duty and obedience been as strong as his filial affection, he would have accused his mother of injustice, and useless caution in thus long withholding from him the secret of his birth: but the grateful tenderness of Edward's heart, and the pliant yieldingness of his disposition, made him conform to the wishes

wishes of his mother, and even form excuses for a taciturnity which gave him the
most poignant uneasiness.—" A day must
come," thought he, " when caution and
concealment will no longer be necessary.
It is the duty of a child to await with pa-
tience the will and pleasure of a parent."

Such were the sentiments of our young
hero; yet, much as has been said, and
much as has been written, concerning
FEMALE curiosity, not one of the most
curious of that curious sex ever longed
more ardently to become master of a secret, than did Edward to attain the knowledge of who was his father. Dearly as
he loved and venerated the memory of his
adopted parent, the kind, the good, the
affectionate Mackenzie, still he had a decided objection to passing through life as
his son, not because that worthy and in-
estimable man had attained no higher rank
in the army than that of a lieutenant, but
because Edward hated every species of deception, and felt the most unconquerable
aversion

aversion to giving utterance to a wilful falsehood.

The more he mixed in society, the more reluctance he felt in appearing under a false name, which frequently gave rise to unmeaning questions concerning his connexions and relatives, which he answered with mingled pain and confusion. What connexions, what relatives had he to boast of? The humbleness of his mother's origin, though it could not weaken his filial love, nevertheless brought the blush of wounded pride on his cheek, as experience taught him the daily lesson, that *appearances* are every thing in what is called the WORLD, and that many of his titled and wealthy acquaintances would change the smile of admiration to the sneer of contempt, were they to learn that the object of their notice was the son of Alice, the humble attendant of the marchioness of Anendale—nay, the marchioness herself, so at least he was taught to believe, would in that

that case become his persecutor—his dead-
ly enemy.

Singular as it may appear, yet this
strange avowal of his mother had no power
to abate the romantic idolatry of the enthusiast Edward. His sudden and mysterious affection for the marchioness was
proof against every thing but her own barbarity; and his heart, which was fearless
of personal danger, was still open to the
genuine emotions of pity, compassion, and
well-grounded, though short-lived resentment. To him, who sacredly revered all
the claims of kindred and friends, the
cruel and unfeminine counsel of lady Anendale to his mother appeared so unnatural,
so barbarous, that in the first impulse of
his horror and his anger, he believed it impossible that he should ever bring himself
to look on her again, or listen with composure to the sound of her name. But
time convinced him that the emotions of
anger are transient in some bosoms, and
that

that his was among the number who warmly feel, and who as quickly forgive an injury, when it is a personal one.

If the blush of pride too often heightened the glow upon the cheek of Edward
at the recollection of his mother's origin,
it was not lessened by the remembrance
of her daughter. It is true that he had a
sister, and that that sister was the child of
him who was one of the kindest, best of
human beings. Yet this sister had never
sent to him the slightest token of acknow-
ledgment, had never written to him, or, as
he had heard, ever expressed the remotest
wish to begin a correspondence, or to receive from him the assurances of his frater-
nal regard.

This cold and heartless conduct, from
one whom Edward felt inclined to love
with all the tenderness of brotherly affection, pained him deeply. The child of
serjeant Mackenzie, independent of any
claim of relationship, could not fail of being
adored

adored by the grateful son of his adoption;
and Edward had often sighed to behold
her, had often longed to embrace her, but
in this he was also doomed to be severely
disappointed.

Since his mother's return to Scotland,
Edward had more than once urged his
wish of being permitted to see Janet Mackenzie; but his mother always framed some
fresh excuse to delay his journey, as well
as to account for the silence of Janet, who
she said was not allowed to answer his letters, her aunt having expressed her dislike to her corresponding with her brother,
lest her thoughts and affections should be
too much engrossed, and diverted from
the objects of her aunt's family.

Edward could hardly repress his indig-
nation at this selfish and narrow-minded
caution of Mrs. Cameron; yet, as his sister
had been reared under her roof, and educated by her at a great expence, he restrained his feelings, lest they should injure

jure the future prospects of Janet, whom he considered to be domesticated for life in the family of her aunt.

Mrs. Mackenzie, who, at the request of Edward, wrote constantly to assure him of her welfare, now appeared to have become tolerably reconciled to the estrangement of her daughter's affections. She seemed to have placed her own upon the eldest Miss Cameron, a girl of seventeen, and whose attention and tenderness promised to make amends for the want of filial love in her own child.

Her first letter to Edward, after her return to the residence of Mrs. Cameron, contained a fear that her daughter was secretly averse to the proposed union with her cousin, Colin Cameron; but the next letter which Edward received tranquillized his mind on this point, and assured him that his mother had been deceived, and that his sister had no objection to the match.

" From her childhood," said Mrs. Mac-

kenzie, " she has been considered as one of the Camerons. Her first affections were taught to fix on the objects by which she was continually surrounded. It would be therefore a pity to disturb the long-formed plans of her aunt, or to attempt to divide the mind of Janet between the friends of her infancy and the brother whom she has never seen since a baby, and whose name she has never heard mentioned by any of the Cameron family. I must content myself, therefore, dear Edward, to relinquish my claim to the heart of my daughter, and turn for comfort and consolation to you, and to my eldest niece, Janet Cameron. This warm-hearted girl, who is about the same age as my own Janet, loves me with a degree of tenderness which reminds me of yourself. She is what I think *you* would call handsome, for her features eternally remind me of those of my dear departed husband. She has been well educated, and plays and sings extremely well; but there is a kindness,
a warmth

a warmth of feeling in her quick and sparkling eye, which is a dark blue, like that of her uncle Mackenzie, which speaks immediately to the soul. Janet Cameron has little or nothing of the Scotch accent: but as I hope that I shall be able to prevail on her mother to let her accompany me back to England, I will not raise your expectations, Edward, too high, lest my young favourite should fall short of them; yet I would fain bespeak your regard for one who already feels towards yourself the kindest sentiments of a relation."

Edward, thus prepared to find in Miss Cameron the dear resemblance of his adopted father, felt an earnest desire to behold *her* who, from that circumstance alone, possessed a strong and sacred claim upon his heart.

Each succeeding letter from his mother increased this desire, till at length he became as anxious to obtain a sight of Janet Cameron, as Frederic Manningham was

to

to gain a glimpse of the secluded daughter of the marchioness of Anendale.

From Frederic Edward had no concealments; a mutual confidence existed between them, and young Manningham was therefore perfectly acquainted with the general theme of Mrs. Mackenzie's correspondence—the name of Janet Cameron was become as familiar to him as that of his own sister, and he felt an interest in her fate, because he believed that Edward's heart had adopted her for a relation. He was therefore pleased to learn from Edward, when he called on him, as he had promised at the opera house, that he had just received a letter from his mother, which gave him hopes that he should see her shortly in London, and that Miss Cameron would accompany her in her journey.

This gratifying intelligence gave fresh animation to the lively spirits of Edward, while those of Frederic were equally exhilarated

hilarated by the promise of his friend to be
ready to proceed into Monmouthshire on
the following morning, as his picture was
now finished, and the money ready to be
remitted to Mr. Curwen by that night's
post. Frederic had also his piece of intelligence to communicate, which was the arrival of his brother Charles and his bride.
They had taken a house only two streets
off from the residence of sir Charles, which
had given great offence to lady Manningham, who was therefore but very ill inclined to receive the new married pair, when
they should think fit to pay her a visit.
Charles had called on the night of his arrival, but all the family were from home,
and Frederic was consequently in expectation of hearing, on his return, that the
visit had been made during his absence.

Edward, though unwilling to touch
upon a subject which would awaken all
the sorrows of Mr. Lindsay, yet felt it his
duty to mention to him the arrival of his

daughter

daughter in London, lest he should be suddenly surprised by her appearance.

It was the good fortune of Edward to possess that pleasing art of softening the most disagreeable intelligence, and Mr. Lindsay received the unwelcome news with a composure which Edward did not expect that he had acquired.

"My dearest Edward," said the father of Clara, "it would not surprise me if Mrs. Manningham was to attempt an interview with me: but I am immoveable in my determination: never will I consent to hold the slightest intercourse with her, until I feel that I am quitting this world. On my deathbed I may once more behold *her* who so cruelly abandoned the best and kindest of mothers—on my deathbed I may bestow on her my forgiveness, but not till then. Edward, I trust to you, and you alone, to save me from the heart-rending agony of seeing my unfeeling child. I shall rely on your precautions,

tions, and on the zeal and affection of the worthy Oliver, who, during your occasional absence, will guard and preserve me from a trial which I am not equal to sustain."

Edward immediately offered to give up his intended journey to Monmouthshire, but this Mr. Lindsay would not allow.—" No, my dear boy," said he, embracing him as he spoke, " I cannot permit you to be an unnecessary sufferer by my misfortunes. I know how much your heart is fixed on delivering into the hands of lady Elinor the packet of her brother, and I will not listen for a moment to the proposal of your giving up your journey on my account. Besides, I cannot always have you with me, and Oliver will faithfully obey my wishes during your absence."

Edward, who was that day engaged to dine with sir Joseph Rennie, thought it advisable to speak to Oliver upon this painful subject.

He accordingly took the opportunity

while

while he was dressing to go out, to inform Oliver of the arrival of Clara, and of the resolution which her father had formed of not seeing her, should she call and attempt an interview.

Oliver, who most sincerely respected as well as pitied his old master, and detested his daughter for her barbarity, promised faithfully to keep watch, lest even the sound of her voice should reach the ears of Mr. Lindsay in his retirement; and Edward, convinced that he might safely rely on the vigilance and attachment of Oliver, felt no scruples in leaving the house and its melancholy inmate to his care.

Sir Joseph Rennie was too much the real friend of Edward, not too feel delighted at the prospect so newly opened to him of acquiring both wealth and fame, from the generous and liberal proposal of Mr. Colvill. He promised to explain this new engagement to the gentleman to whom he was about to introduce him, in such a manner

manner as would prevent his taking offence at Edward's declining, for the present, to paint his altar-piece.

Sir Joseph congratulated Edward upon his acquiring the friendship of the Osborne family, particularly that of Mr. Colvill, the brother of lady James, whose character he had heard from a friend well acquainted with the virtues of both brother and sister.—" But," said sir Joseph, " have you engaged fresh apartments? for those you now occupy, as I have before stated, are not such as you ought to inhabit."

Edward replied that he had taken lodgings in one of the fashionable streets, to which he meant to remove as soon as the returned from a short visit which be was about to make into Monmouthshire.

Sir Joseph naturally expressed a desire to learn the object of his young friend's journey into that county, and Edward made no scruple of confiding to him the truth, as he had been the means of introducing him to the marchioness and her

son, and had since then frequently mentioned the latter in terms of regret, that
authorized Edward to describe to him the
artless tenderness and honourable confidence of the heir of Anendale.

"And you really intend to take a journey on purpose into Monmouthshire," said
sir Joseph, " that you may perform your
promise to the deceased earl? Well, my
dear Mackenzie, I honour you for holding
your word sacred. But how do you pro-
pose to gain admittance to the castle of
the marchioness? You are not perhaps
aware of the extreme vigilance of madame
Dubois, who is the governess of lady Elinor, and who will think it her duty not
to suffer her pupil to hold any communication with a young man of whom she is
wholly ignorant, and whose romantic
errand may authorize her to deem him an
impostor."

Edward replied that he had never once
reflected on the improbability of his being
admitted to see lady Elinor; and though
his

his friend, Frederic Manningham, had agreed to accompany him on his expedition, yet it had never struck either of them that their journey would prove a useless one, or that they should find any difficulty in gaining the good opinion of madame Dubois, through whose interest alone they expected to see lady Elinor.

Sir Joseph smiled at this proof of Edward's ignorance of the world, as it was not very likely that an artful intriguing Frenchwoman, such as he had reason to believe madame Dubois, would suffer her pupil to see and converse with two handsome young men like Edward and his friend Manningham; both of them were by far too attractive in their persons to be introduced to a young, inexperienced, and secluded girl, like lady Elinor.

" I think," said sir Joseph, " that in this dilemma my advice will be serviceable to you, Mackenzie. A little worldly artifice in this case may be resorted to without injury to any one. The marquis of Anen-

dale

dale has added considerably to the picture gallery of lady Fitz-Arthur, as he generally resides at the Castle a part of the summer months, and is not a little proud of his collection of paintings, as well as of being considered as one of the most zealous patrons of the fine arts. It is this collection, Mackenzie, which must be the means of introducing you to the interior of lady Elinor's prison, as well as a note which I will give you to deliver to her watchful duenna, madame Dubois, who is well ac-quainted with my name, as I have been on a visit more than once to the marquis, when he has resided at the Castle, which contains several of my pictures. My name will be the passport to the presence of madame; after that you must trust to chance, or to your own talents at invention, to procure you the accomplishment of your wishes."

' Edward warmly testified his acknowledgments to sir Joseph for thus kindly assisting him in the attainment of his hopes.—

hopes.—" In any other case than the present," said Edward, " I should feel a repugnance to adopting a measure which might subject me hereafter to the imputation of deception: but the motives of my visit seem to justify the means. I promised most solemnly to deliver to lady Elinor the little packet entrusted to me by her brother, and in performing this promise, I cannot perceive any possible harm that can arise from my using an innocent stratagem to procure me the sight of lady Elinor."

" In any other case," replied sir Joseph, gravely, " I should be equally averse to giving my sanction to your wishes; but here I feel no compunction to forward your plan of performing the dying bequest of an affectionate brother, and of bestowing on lady Elinor the melancholy pleasure of receiving the last testimonies of his regard. The marchioness, though dotingly fond of her son, endeavoured to repress as much as possible his tenderness

for

for his sister, whom she treated with indifference, keeping her the chief of the day to her studies, that she might not have the opportunity of associating with her brother. Notwithstanding this cruel attempt to disunite them, nature in their young and innocent bosoms would have its course, and they seemed to love each other in proportion to the pains which was taken to render them careless and neglectful. The marchioness was proof to all the tender pleadings of her son on his last removal from the Castle, and decidedly opposed the wishes of the marquis and his heir, which were to have lady Elinor accompany them to town. The poor boy seemed conscious of his approaching dissolution, and asked leave to bestow on his sister a lock of his hair: but this boon the marchioness had sufficient firmness to refuse. Had the life of lady Elinor depended on her possessing a ringlet of her brother's hair, her mother would not have allowed one of those precious curls to have

Have been dissevered from his head. I can only account for lady Anendale's conduct towards her daughter, by supposing that she fears that the novelty of a fresh face, intelligent, innocent, and more youthful than her own, may steal from her a portion of that unbounded admiration which she still continues to excite in the breasts of her numerous followers."

" How groundless this fear!", exclaimed Edward, with warmth; " how improbable that any man who once had viewed the lovely graces, the matchless beauties of the marchioness, should quit her side, or exchange her smiles for those of her daughter !"

Sir Joseph frowned for a moment on the young enthusiast, but his face quickly recovered its wonted serenity, as he considered that youth and inexperience were not proof against the dangerous combination of female beauty and female artifice.

" Mackenzie," said sir Joseph, with his accustomed kindness, as he laid his hand

on

on his shoulder, " Mackenzie, I am almost tempted to believe that you are in
love with the marchioness of Anendale:
Of this I am sure, that you are one of her
warmest admirers."

"In love with the marchioness of Anendale!" cried Edward, in a tone of surprise, yet with a look of the deepest confusion : " no, sir Joseph, I am not in love
with the marchioness, though I am certain
that no other woman in the world could
ever give birth to the same emotions in
my heart as she has done."

" I own the magic of her charms," replied sir Joseph; " but my knowledge of
her character has shielded me from their
siren influence. I have seen lady Elinor,
of whose beauty you have formed so slight
an opinion. When you return, Mackenzie, from Monmouthshire, you will perhaps prefer the daughter's unstudied graces
to the tempting allurements of the mother's practised graces. Guard well your
heart, lest, if still unoccupied, it should
                                        admit

admit an image, whose modesty and self-taught virtues may eclipse the dazzling lustre of maturer beauties."

Edward was not sorry to be now interrupted by the arrival of company, which afforded a seasonable relief to his feelings. He quickly recovered his vivacity and self-command — not that he could wholly dismiss from his mind the conversation of sir Joseph, or the approaching interview which he hoped to gain with lady Elinor.

The day, however, passed most agreeably with our young artist, whose talents were not confined alone to the pencil; they shone alike in conversation, in which he displayed taste, wit, and judgment, far above his years; and when he rose to take leave, that he might call on Mr. Colvill, the guests of sir Joseph felt a momentary blank at his departure, which they endeavoured to fill up by sounding the praises of so young a man, whose superior understanding, good-natured wit, and extensive knowledge.

knowledge, had afforded to all present the highest satisfaction.

It was late before Edward returned home from Osborne House. He had found Mr. Colvill alone and indisposed, and he had therefore staid longer than he had intended, as he had a few arrangements to make preparatory to his leaving town the next morning. As soon as he had entered his own apartments, Oliver presented him with a letter, which he said he was sure came from Miss Clara, as he knew her hand-writing as well as he did his own.

Oliver was right; the letter was indeed from the pen of Mrs. Manningham, who earnestly besought Edward to call upon her as soon as possible. Ungrateful and unfeeling as she was, Edward immediately determined to hasten to her residence, in the generous hope of finding her repentant of her past conduct, and anxious to make every atonement in her power for the faults which she had committed.

How great, therefore, was the disappointment

appointment of Edward the moment he beheld Mrs. Manningham! Instead of the penitent daughter which he had expected to meet, he was received by the gay and lively bride of Charles, with as free an air, as careless a manner, as if she had no one sin of which her conscience could accuse her.

" This visit is doubly kind of you, Edward," said she, offering him her cheek, which he coldly saluted, " as my servant informed me that you were from home when he left my letter, and I had therefore given you up for to-night: to-morrow I expected to have seen you."

" To-morrow I leave town for a few days," replied Edward, " and as I thought that you might have a particular wish to see me as soon as you came to town, I hurried here the instant I received your letter, although the lateness of the hour might have excused my absence."

" I thank you," said Clara, " for this
proof

proof of your forgiveness. We parted, Edward, in mutual displeasure; but let that be forgotten. I almost wish now that I had taken your advice, for Charles has considerable doubts respecting the liquidation of his debts; and his temper, which was always impetuous, is not mended by the prospect of doing penance for what the old people term his imprudent marriage. Manningham saw them last night, and would fain have persuaded me to accompany him there to-day; but I do not intend to expose myself to the taunts and reproaches of his lady-mother, or the paternal advice of his sermonizing father. Time will convince them that I am neither a child nor a fool, and that I shall be able to pass through life very well without their countenance and support."

Edward, shocked by this speech, as well as disgusted with the speaker, replied, that he should have supposed, that for her own sake, as well as her husband's, she

she would have sought to obtain a reconciliation with his parents.

"I shall not stoop to beg for their favours," said Mrs. Manningham, "as I consider myself the equal of their son; and should they refuse to advance him the money to pay his debts, why, we must make up our minds to go abroad, which will not be at all disagreeable to me, who have no one in England to regret or to care about leaving."

Edward fixed his eyes on the unblushing countenance of Clara. His looks spoke volumes; and for a moment she felt abashed.—" *Your* FATHER, Mrs. Manningham, still lives!" exclaimed Edward, in a tone of bitter reproach.

" True; but my father has refused to open my letters; he has forgotten *me*— why then should I remember *him*?"

Edward rose indignantly from his seat; he was no longer master of his feelings or of his temper.—" I see," said he, " that my visit was unnecessary. You can have no
wish

wish to hold any further communication
with one who thinks and feels in every
respect so opposite to yourself."

" Is this a proof of your gratitude?"
exclaimed Clara, angrily—" is this the
return for all. my past kindness towards
you? What inducement could I have to
send for you, Mackenzie, but to prove that
I was still inclined to consider you as my
friend and brother? Have you then quite
forgotten all my former affection, when
you were an inmate of your grandmother's cottage, that thus you defy my
resentment and slight my friendship?"

" The readiness with which I obeyed
your summons proves," replied Edward,
" that I am not in the habit of forgetting
any kindness which I have received, either
from *you* or your worthy and affectionate
*parents*. Your mother breathed her last
sigh in my arms, as she invoked a blessing
upon the head of that child who had deserted her in her last moments; and your
poor afflicted father, though nearly lost to
all

all the enjoyments of life, still finds comfort and support from the testimonies of my gratitude and love. . Death deprived *me* of a home and of a relation who adored me. Your father, Mrs. Manningham, generously did his utmost to make up for the loss which I had sustained: he was my friend, my father, my benefactor; and now, when death has deprived *him* of the only tie, the only solace of his existence, I feel it an imperious duty, as well as a grateful pleasure, that I should devote myself to his service, that I should assuage his anguish, compose his mind, and be to him a son, since he no longer possesses the affection of his daughter." ·

. A momentary feeling of remorse entered the heart of Clara.—" Stay, Edward," said she, laying her hand on his arm; " I cannot resist the force of that power you have always held over me. I would fain be restored to the bosom of my father, but I cannot bring myself to meet with a repulse,

pulse, even from *him*. Will he see me at *your* request?"

' Edward shook his head.—" I will not deceive you," he replied: " your father feels too deeply, too acutely, your conduct to the tenderest of mothers, ever to listen to anything like an interview with you, unless he was on the point of death. At that awful moment his resentment may abate, and he may once more receive you to his arms; but until then, all attempts at a reconciliation will be fruitless. It is a subject which I am commanded to abstain from, and I feel it my duty not to add to his distress by the mention of your name. If I am thus compelled to speak unwelcome truths, you must blame circumstances, not me. It was my wish to serve you, my warmest desire to save you from the bitterness of an accusing conscience; but you would not let me exert the privileges of a brother, which you yourself had formerly given to me."

Mrs.

Mrs. Manninghan looked as if she felt for once in her life for some one not herself.—" Will you call on me when you return to town, Edward ?" said she ; " I shall always be happy to see you, notwithstanding the difference of our thoughts and opinions."

Edward gave a reluctant consent, and then hurried back to the temporary abode of her deserted parent, his heart kindling towards him with redoubled tenderness, as he felt more than ever the sad conviction that no hope remained of his receiving any consolation in this world from the child of his fondest affections, his misplaced idolatry!—" Poor Mr. Lindsay !" sighed Edward, " how unbounded was thy love!—how base has been its return!"

Fortunately for Edward, the appearance of Oliver gave a seasonable turn to his ideas, and his mind gradually became occupied by the more pleasing subject of the next day's journey to the castle of the marchioness of Anendale.

# CHAPTER X.

IT had been the first intention of Edward
and his friend Manningham to make as
rapid a journey as possible into Monmouthshire, that their stay might not exceed a
limited time; but they now altered their
plan, allowing themselves a day or two
to look round them, and to examine whatever was worthy of their inspection in the
route they meant to take.

They were both at that delightful age
when the mind catches at every distant
ray of pleasure, and the heart swells with
rapture at the fairy visions of its own crea-
tion. Season of bliss, how short is your
duration! how transient your enjoyments!

Spring had already put forth her varied
charms; the fields could boast of their un-
wearying verdure, and the trees and shrubs
of

of their changeful. foliage; all nature seemed teeming with delight; and the joyous faces of the lively peasantry, as they sung or whistled their favourite provincial airs during the labours of the day, added to the cheerfulness of the scene, and to the hilarity of the travellers.

"We are a couple of fine fellows truly, Mackenzie," said Frederic, gaily, as they were taking their dinner at one of the best inns in Monmouthshire; " here we are, safe from all the neck-break disasters of the road, and upwards of a hundred and twenty miles from any human being that we know. If this lady Elinor should prove not worth the trouble we have taken to get a sight of her, how mortified we shall both feel at our romantic expedition !"

" Not at all, my dear friend," replied Edward, smilingly; " my purpose here is merely to perform the promise which I gave to her brother; that accomplished, I shall return satisfied. Should the ardour of your passion abate upon an interview

L 2

with

with its object, you must fortify your mind with the reflection that your journey will not altogether be an unpleasing one; and that many a bright eye in London will sparkle with delight, should your *romantic expedition* prove a fruitless one. Come, fill again your glass, friend of my soul; let us once more drink to the health, happiness, and speedy emancipation of the daughter of lady Anendale."

"And may we find her just the same lovely, modest, artless, bashful, yet warm-hearted girl that my imagination has pictured her to be! To any other man than yourself, Mackenzie, I should be almost ashamed to acknowledge what may be a proof of my bad taste; but there is a certain something which I look in vain to find in the manners and persons of our young women of fashion—a something which I feel to be indispensable in the woman whom I may select as the partner of my future life. I see that you do *not* smile, Mackenzie, at my fastidiousness,

and

and that you think and feel as I do, not-withstanding," added he, archly, "your recent gallantry to lady Jane ——. I cannot tell why, but I have taken it into my mad brain, that this neglected daughter of your earthly divinity will exactly suit my taste. But why do we waste the precious moments, which might be otherwise employed? Let us hasten to the castle of her mother—ply her duenna with well-timed flattery—gain her confidence, and by that means ensure to ourselves a sight of the most valuable picture in the possession of the marquis."

Frederic now rang to inquire if fresh horses were put to the carriage, and on being told that they were, the young men proceeded with buoyant spirits to the venerable mansion, which Frederic termed the prison-house of lady Elinor.

As they approached the castle of Fitz-Arthur, Manningham felt his appellation to be just. It was a place which had formerly been of considerable strength; gloo-

my

my and awfully grand, it seemed to mock
the ravages of time, which were visible in-
some parts of the building, that were wash-
ed by the waves of a bold and beautiful
river.. The postillion stopped at the massy
gate of the castle, which was opened (not
with the speed of a Mercury), by an old
man who appeared to fill the office of porter, and to whom Edward delivered the
letter for madame Dubois, from sir Joseph
Rennie. Nearly a quarter of an hour
elapsed before the return of the hobbling
old porter, and they were then requested
to alight, while another domestic, somewhat younger, and a little more agile, conducted them to the presence of madame.

The eyes of the Frenchwoman examined with scrutinizing attention the counte-
nances of her visitors, as she in broken English asked them a variety of questions, which
she conceived to be of importance, before
she consented to the request of sir Joseph,
and allowed them to view the interior of
the principal apartments of the Castle, of
which

which she was deputed sole mistréss during the absence of its noble owners. The handsome persons of Edward and Frederic, their polite apologies for not making her an earlier visit, lest they had now intruded on her time, and their manly and elegant forms, so won upon the favour of madame, that she invited them to be her guests for the night, saying, that as the day was far spent, they could not possibly have time to form a just opinion of the splendid collection of the marquis of Anendale; she had a high respect for sir Joseph Rennie, and would do all in her power to entertain his friends.

The young men, scarce able to conceal their joy, most willingly gave orders for the dismissal of their chaise, returning madame many flattering compliments for her kind attention to the object of their visit; to which she replied, that she should be extremely happy to afford them every possible gratification, as their appearance and manners justified her in so doing.

Neither

Neither Edward nor Frederie were backward in making the proper acknowledgments for the condescension and kindness of madame, who, on her part, seemed highly delighted with her young and handsome guests, quickly giving them to understand that she rejoiced at the circumstance which had conducted them to the castle, and complaining bitterly of the dull life which she led during the absence of its owners.

In the hope of being rewarded by a sight of lady Elinor, the friends lavished on the wily Frenchwoman compliments and attentions which would have disgusted the purity of English education : but madame received the grossest flattery with a greediness which proved the corruption of her mind, and the impurity of her morals. Her guests, though young, instantly comprehended the character of madame Dubois; and while the sincerity of their nature recoiled from the base prostitution of their praise, they felt convinced that all hope

hope of seeing lady Elinor was vain, unless they could charm and amuse her unprincipled duenna.

Madame, though perfectly enchanted with her youthful visitors, and with Edward in particular, was not unmindful of the important charge committed to her care. She laughed and talked with a freedom which gave licence to the boldest thoughts; yet, if she gave way to the levity of her disposition, she still remembered that to her was entrusted the only child of the marquis of Anendale. After indulging herself in the pleasures of conversation, she apologized for being obliged to leave them for a few minutes.

" And is this the being," exclaimed Frederic warmly, " to whom the sacred trust is delegated of forming the mind and morals of an English girl? Can any thing prove more strongly the unpardonable negligence of the marchioness, than this one act of misplaced confidence? What can

we

we expect from the pupil of madame Dubois?"

"Nay, my dear friend," said Edward, "suffer not the warmth of your present feelings to lead you into error. Lady Elinor may have escaped from the contagion of precept and example; the purity of her mind may have shielded her from the knowledge of that profligacy which is so apparent in that of her governess—at least, it is but charitable in us to think so, until we know to the contrary."

"Alas!" cried Frederic, in a tone of real commiseration, "it is vain to cheat myself with so delusive a hope. Lady Elinor is the daughter of the marchioness, and the pupil of madame Dubois."

"I have never heard any thing against the moral character of the marchioness," replied Edward hastily; "and as to the levity now displayed in the conduct of madame, it does not prove that she is equally unguarded when in the company of lady Elinor.

imaginary evils. We shall most likely be
honoured by a sight of her ladyship, when

an estimate of her character."

pointment of Frederic, on beholding in lady

.

the heart. A visible confusion seemed to
increase the awkwardness of lady Elinor;

she

she curtsied ungracefully to the mortified
friends, then hastily seated herself close by
the side of madame, whose watchful glances
vainly endeavoured to inspire her pupil
with confidence and encouragement.

Lady Elinor took no part in the conversation, which now became too dull for the
lively thoughts of madame. She rallied
the young men upon their sudden thought-
fulness, imputing it to the recollection of
their mistresses, whom they had left behind—" I have a few orders to give to our
old housekeeper," said she, "which will detain me from you perhaps half-an-hour. In
the meanwhile lady Elinor shall conduct
you to one of the picture-galleries; and, by
the time that I join you, I shall expect to
find you as gay and as animated as you
were before I left you."

She then desired her embarrassed pupil
to shew the gentlemen to the southern gallery, which contained only a part of the
pictures belonging to the collection of lady
Fitz-Arthur. Lady Elinor slowly obeyed,
                                        and

and our two friends as slowly followed her
footsteps. Edward's mind had not long
to dwell upon the disappointment which
both himself and Frederic had received.
He was now within the walls of the castle
which had sheltered his mother from childhood unto womanhood—of that castle which
had also been the chief residence of the fascinating marchioness, and in whose spaci-
ous and magnificent apartments her infant
family had first seen the light. All that
now remained of her numerous offspring
was lady Elinor—a being so entirely unlike either father or mother, that Edward
could not bring himself to believe that she
was the child of the beautiful lady Anendale. Yet, as he gazed with doubtful
wonder upon her ladyship, he no longer
felt surprised at the mother's reluctance to
introduce into the world such a compound
of stiffness, awkwardness, and inelegance.

Notwithstanding the mortified feelings
of Edward, he was neither insensible to
the valuable paintings which adorned the
southern

southern gallery, nor careless of the present opportunity of delivering to lady Elinor the packet of her deceased brother. With some share of emotion, he explained to her ladyship the manner in which he had become possessed of the packet, which contained the hair of the young earl, and his surprise was considerably increased by the little feeling which she displayed upon an occasion when he had expected to see her bathed in tears, and warm in gratitude to him who had undertaken so long a journey entirely for her sake, that she might receive the last testimony of her brother's affectionate remembrance. Lady Elinor received the packet with painful confusion; put it hastily into her pocket, and stammered out a few inaudible words, which Edward supposed were thanks for his kindness. That she might recover from an embarrassment for which he could not account, he now turned his attention to the pictures, in order that she might have time to recover her composure.

When

When madame rejoined them, lady Elinor retired, as Edward conjectured, to examine the contents of her packet, but in reality from a far different motive, which at that moment our hero little imagined. The gaiety of madame, her sprightly *badinage*, and her flattering compliments, soon recalled the flagging spirits of the two

the most of what amusement lay in their way, and to cast aside, if possible, all remembrance of the severe disappointment which each had received from their interview with lady Elinor, and to make themselves as agreeable as they could to madame, who, on her part, appeared anxious to afford them every gratification which rested on her own powers of pleasing.

Madame Dubois was just turned of nine-and-twenty; she was handsome, well-shaped, and abounding with wit and anecdote; she possessed all the levity of her country-women—all their frivolity and heartless coquetry, without any of their good qualities.

A perfect

A perfect adept at intrigue, she determined to practise all her arts upon her present guests, hoping to fix the attention of one or the other, no matter which, though she would have given the preference to Edward; and thus, if possible, secure to herself a more pleasing establishment than the dependent one she now held in the family of the marquis.

At tea lady Elinor again appeared for a few minutes. She looked as if she wished for an opportunity to speak to Edward; but none occurred, and she therefore withdrew, by the desire of her governess, who felt no inclination to have any one present who could be a spy over her words and actions. Upon learning that the young men were fond of music, she entertained them with several of her own national airs ; and as she sung well, and played still better, they listened to her with satisfaction; expressing themselves with a degree of warmth which repaid the exertions of madame.

On retiring for the night, madame hoped that

that their slumbers would not be disturbed
by the dashing of the water against that
part of the castle where their chambers lay.
She added, that it might be necessary to tell
them this, lest they should misconstrue the
monotonous sound into the moaning voice
of some unquiet spirit, who was the necessary inmate of every old mansion in the
world. Then, reminding them of their promise of rising early the next morning, that
they might accompany her over the principal rooms of the castle, and from thence
into the grounds, she reluctantly took leave
of her interesting guests, whom she now
consigned to the care of a venerable-look-
ing old woman, whom they were given to
understand was the housekeeper of the
castle.

This ancient domestic, enfeebled by age,
and nearly deprived of sight, ascended
slowly, and with the help of a crutch, the
noble flight of marble stairs which led to
the several bedchambers, and best apartments

ments of the house. 'Edward, in whom
the appearance of age never failed to excite
respect, good-naturedly obliged his conduc-
tress to accept of his support, apologizing
for the trouble which his presence occasioned her.

At the sound of his voice the old woman suddenly stopped, and, as she pressed
his arm with additional weight, curiously
and anxiously endeavoured to run over the
features of Edward's face; but her dim
eyes refused to discover to her the sight
she wished, and again she tottered forward,
until she entered a long gloomy passage,
partially enlightened by a lamp, which was
suspended from the middle of the ceiling.
At the extremity of the gallery were the
rooms which had been prepared for the visitors, one of which she pointed out to Frederic as being destined to receive him, and
then followed Edward into the next.

'" Sit down and rest yourself," said Edward, in a tone of compassionate kindness.
" I hope

" I hope it is not often that your strength is thus exhausted, by ascending so high a flight of stairs."

" Oh, that sweet, sweet voice !" exclaimed the old woman, as she seated herself in a chair, and still holding by the arm of Edward, who began to feel a something more than casual veneration for his companion. " What would I now give," she continued, " could I but see if your face is as like as your voice is to that dear kind soul, whom I have so often hugged and kissed when a boy ! Ah, sir, you must pardon the freedom of an old woman like me; but my heart danced again with joy, as it was used to do when that person spoke to me, the moment that I heard the sound of your voice. Who knows but you may be a relation of his ? and yet your name——"

" Is Mackenzie," replied Edward, with some degree of emotion.

" Ah, then you are no relation, and perhaps not at all like him, only your voice. Well,

Well, I am now in my seventy-fifth year,
and when I last saw him I was fifty-five.
God knows I little dreamed that it was for
the last time.—' Bridget Carter,' said he,
taking me round the neck, and kissing me
with the kindness of a son, '.Bridget Carter, I am compelled: to leave Monmouthshire immediately. Keep this box,' and it
was a silver snuff-box, ' for my sake—until I return, keep it, Bridget, as sacredly as
you would the good name of your beautiful mistress.'. And Bridget has kept them
both as sacred as he, dear soul, could wish;
but Bridget has never set eyes on him from
that day to this."

"You have lived many years in this
castle, I suppose," said Edward; ", and
must therefore be tenderly attached to the
marchioness and her children?"

"Only one remains, only one remains,"
cried the old woman hastily, " out of eight
as lovely babes as ever saw the light. The
righteous Judge of all has thus thought
fit to visit upon the marchioness the in-
constancy

constancy of her early youth. Yes, I have
lived long, very long, in the castle. I was
nurse to lady Fitz-Arthur; and when she
died, her niece wished me to remain as housekeeper. So, as I had passed so much of my
life at the castle, I thought best to smother
my feelings, and not seek a fresh home in
the days of my old age. My lady soon
married after the death of her aunt, but I
said to myself, that no good would come to
one who had so cruelly deceived one of the
best and kindest men on earth."

"The marchioness was then in love with
the person to whom you allude?" said Edward.

"In love! God keep me from such
love!" exclaimed the old woman fervently.
"Why, you must know, sir—Mercy on
me! I could almost fancy that I was speaking to him now; but that I know cannot
be the case, for I dare say he died bro-
kenhearted, poor, dear soul! when he
heard of my lady's marriage with the marquis! And as for me, I almost cried myself
blind

blind with pure grief at the thought of what he would suffer; but my lady was as gay and as thoughtless as ever, so she made out the words of our worthy old Margaret Grey—' An Angel's form and a Devil's heart,' for sure enough she has both."

Edward gave an involuntary start at the mention of his grandmother's name, and Bridget Carter, not noticing his agitation, went on with her story.

" Well, as I was saying, when my lady was quite a young thing in her teens, she took it into her head to be desperately in love with a young gentleman, who used to spend part of his holidays with a relation in Monmouthshire. They saw each other by accident, and though then only boy and girl, took a liking to each other. Well, what was to be done? Lady FitzArthur and his uncle had quarrelled about a piece of land, and hated each other like poison; so the young folks knew they could only see each other by stealth. My lady

lady was very infirm for some years before her death, and this gave her niece opportunity to meet her lover as often as she pleased and he had time, in the filbert-walk, on the east side of the castle garden. I was the first to find them out; but I no sooner cast my eyes, for I could see then as well as any-body, on his fine, open, manly face, than I thought to myself, 'twas no wonder at Miss Fitz-Arthur falling in love with it; and when he took my hand and told me who he was, and begged me not to betray him, the very sound of his voice seemed to do my heart good, and I promised solemnly never to tell my lady of any of their stolen interviews. Well, year after year went by, and still they met as usual, and still my old heart danced with delight at the sound of his voice; for next to seeing my young lady, he always contrived to see me; and many and many a kiss have I had from his sweet lips, and many a prayer have I called down upon his dear head. Ah! this very room was the

bed-

bed-chamber of Miss Fitz-Arthur when she was a girl; *that* was her bed, and *that* her toilet, and that very bookcase, I dare say, has often and often concealed his letters."

Edward cast a glance round the apartment; his heart beat quicker than usual, and every word uttered by Bridget Carter added to the strangeness of his newly-awakened feelings. He would not have interrupted her for the world.

"Between those cabinets," said she, "is a door, which is now fastened up by order of the marchioness, but which then was serviceable to the lovers. It communicates by a long flight of steps to the river, which sometimes overflows nearly half of them, and by these her lover used to gain admittance to her chamber, when he could not see her in any other place. I did not like this way of their meeting; but I was old, they were young, and my lady would have her own way; but I often told Alice that no good would come if they met in that way."

"Alice!"

"Alice!" exclaimed Edward, tremblingly, "who was Alice?"

"Alice was old Margaret's daughter by her first husband," said Bridget, without noticing the strange inquiry of Edward, or his increasing emotion—"Margaret was housekeeper to lady Fitz-Arthur until she married Grey; and when she left, Alice remained to attend upon and to amuse my young lady, who was very fond of her, and who took a great deal of pains to make Alice fit to be her companion. My lady also was partial to the girl, so she made no objection, and so Alice by this means got an education above her situation. But she was a kind, warm-hearted girl, and we all loved her, and all felt sorry when she left the castle, though we often said, among each other, that it was a pity my young lady had got such power over her."

"I suppose she left the castle because she was married?" said Edward, tremblingly.

"Married! no, no, Alice was not mar-

ried when she left the castle," said Bridget.
" Poor girl ! Heaven only knows what has
become, of her; from that day to this we
have never heard any tidings of poor Alice,
but we suspected——"

At that instant a sudden movement in
the gallery was heard by Bridget, who rising with tolerable quickness, motioned to
Edward to be silent, and then left the
chamber, with the cautious tread and scrutinizing glance of experienced age.

**END OF VOL. III.**

Printed by J. Darling, Leadenhall-Street, London.

# NEW PUBLICATIONS

PRINTED FOR

## A. K. NEWMAN & CO.

AT THE

### Minerva=Press,

## LEADENHALL-STREET, LONDON.

———

|  | £ | s. | d. |
|---|---|---|---|
| Baron of Falconberg, or Childe Harolde in Prose, by Bridget Bluemantle, 3 vols. | 0 | 15 | 0 |
| Dangerous Secrets, a Scottish Tale, 2 vols. | 0 | 10 | 6 |
| Theresa, or the Wizard's Fate, 4 vols. | 1 | 2 | 0 |
| Celebrity, by Mrs. Pilkington, 3 vols. | 0 | 15 | 0 |
| Border Chieftains, by Miss Houghton, 2d edition, 3 vols. | 0 | 18 | 0 |
| Barozzi, or the Venetian Sorceress, a Romance, by Mrs. Smith, Author of the Caledonian Bandit, &c. 2 vols. | 0 | 10 | 6 |
| Duncan and Peggy, a Scottish Tale, by Mrs. Helme, new edition, 3 vols. | 0 | 15 | 0 |
| Discontented Man, by A. F. Holstein, 3 vols. | 0 | 16 | 6 |
| Vaga, or a View of Nature, by Mrs. Peck, 2d edition, 3 vols. | 0 | 18 | 0 |
| Lady Jane's Pocket, by the Author of Silvanella, 4 vols. | 1 | 2 | 0 |
| The Bristol Heiress, by Mrs. Sleath, Author of the Orphan of the Rhine, &c. 5 vols. | 1 | 5 | 0 |
| Family Estate, or Lost and Won, by Mrs. Ross, Author of Modern Calypso, &c. &c. 3 vols. | 0 | 15 | 0 |
| Donald Monteith, the Handsomest Man of the Age, by Selma Davenport, Author of the Sons of the Viscount and the Daughters of the Earl, and the Hypocrite, 5 vols. | 1 | 5 | 0 |
| Romantic Facts, or Which is his Wife? 4 vols. | 1 | 2 | 0 |
| Emmeline, or the Orphan of the Castle, by Charlotte Smith, new edition, 4 vols. | 1 | 2 | 0 |

|                                                                                 | £ | s. | d. |
|---------------------------------------------------------------------------------|---|----|----|
| Sons of St. David, a Cambro-British Historical Romance, by Griffiths ap Griffiths, Esq. 3 vols.. | 0 | 15 | 0 |
| Hermione, or the Defaulter, by Caroline Scott, 2 vols .. | 0 | 10 | 6 |
| Mary and Fanny, by Juvenis | 0 | 4 | 0 |
| Park's Travels in Africa, abridged by John Campbell, Esq. | 0 | 4 | 6 |
| Original of the Miniature, by Selma Davenport, 4 vols . | 1 | 2 | 0 |
| Godfrey Ranger, by D. W. Paynter, 3 vols. | 0 | 16 | 6 |
| Cicely, or the Rose of Raby, by Agnes Musgrave, 3d edition, 4 vols. | | | |
| The Revealer of Secrets, by the Author of Substance and Shadow &c. 3 vols. | 1 | 0 | 0 |
| | 0 | 15 | 0 |
| Claudine, or Pertinacity, by Bridget Bluemantle, 3 vols | 0 | 15 | 0 |
| Villasantelle, or the Curious Impertinent, by Catharine Selden | 0 | 6 | 6 |
| The Wife of Fitzalice and the Caledonian Siren, a Romance, by Marianne Breton, 5 vols. | 1 | 7 | 6 |
| Life of a Recluse, by A. Gibson, 2 vols. | 0 | 10 | 6 |
| Mysteries of Hungary, a Romantic Story of the Fifteenth Century, by Edward Moore, Esq. Author of Sir Ralph de Bigod, &c. &c. 3 vols. | 0 | 16 | 6 |
| Gonzalo de Baldivia, a Romance, by Anne of Swansea, 4 vols. | 1 | 2 | 0 |
| Education, or Elizabeth, her Lover and Husband, by Eliza Taylor, 3 vols. | 0 | 15 | 0 |
| Penitent of Godstow; or Magdalen, by Mrs. Helme, 2d edition, 3 vols | 0 | 15 | 0 |
| St. Clair of the Isles, or the Outlaws of Barra, by the same, 2d edition, 4 vols | 1 | 0 | 0 |
| Caroline of Lichtfield, a new edition, translated by Thomas Holcroft, 3 vols. | 0 | 15 | 0 |
| Memoirs of an American Lady, by the Author of Letters from the Mountains, 3d edition, 2 vols. | 0 | 12 | 0 |
| Love, Hatred, and Revenge, a Swiss Romance, by T. P. Lathy, 2d edition, 3 vols | 0 | 15 | 0 |
| Devil upon Two Sticks in England, by the Author of Dr. Syntax's Tour in Search of the Picturesque, &c. 4th edition, 6 vols. | 1 | 10 | 0 |